MOONLIT AGATE

MOONLIT FALLS, BOOK 8

KATHERINE ISAAC

Moonlit Agate

Copyright © 2021 by Katherine Isaac

This book is a work of fiction. All names, characters, places, and incidents are the products of the author's imagination. Any resemblance to actual events, locales, or actual persons, living or dead, is entirely coincidental.

Cover Art © J.E. Cluney 2021

Editing: Emma Luna at Moonlight Author Services

Proofreading: Kaye Kemp at Kaye Kemp Book Polishing

All rights reserved.

No part of this book may be reproduced in any form or by any electronic or mechanical means, including information storage and retrieval systems, without written permission from the author, except for the use of brief quotations in a book review.

Moon Dust Library

10 9 8 7 6 5 4 3 2 1

To the readers willing to take a chance on a new author

CHAPTER ONE

There was something calming about the sensation of dirt between my toes. It was as if I could feel the heartbeat of the Earth herself reverberating through the soles of my feet. It seemed to center my emotions and strengthen the magic flowing through my veins. Taking a deep breath, the scent of damp soil coursed through my lungs, warming me from the inside.

It was early and unusually chilly for mid-summer. A fine mist was slowly lifting from the forest, revealing dew-touched grass from the night's gentle rain. Looking up at the pale slice of sky peeking out from behind the canopy branches, I smiled to myself. There were no clouds, and all signs pointed to a bright, warm day.

A soft breeze blew through the trees. A mix of green and copper leaves swirled around my bare ankles and gently caressed the wings on my back. Unlike my pointed ears, these four iridescent membranes were rounded at the tips and often lay folded against my spine, much like the wings of a bee. Stretching them out behind me, I lifted slightly onto my toes as I tried to energize myself for the day ahead.

A yawn sounded from behind me as Maeve, my best friend and roommate, slowly walked up to me. Her dark hair was tied haphazardly in a messy bun, flopping to one side, and she gently rubbed the last grains of sleep from the corners of her eyes.

"Was it really necessary to start so early today, or did I do something to annoy you? Whatever it was, I'm really sorry and won't do it again. I promise!"

Giving her one of my signature grins, I took her hand in mine, gently pulling the practically sleep-walking gnome along with me as I started to walk away from our house.

"I admit, I did wait until you were three glasses of wine down before asking you for help on this project. But you know how excited I am!"

"All I heard just now was that you got me drunk before asking me for something I'd regret. I trusted you, Aggy!" Maeve whined good-humoredly as I tugged her along the worn path towards the town.

"Oh, hush, you still trust me. Besides, I should only need your help for the first few days, maybe less if you actually walk instead of making me drag you."

Maeve slumped against me in an almost-hug and groaned. "If you weren't so short, I'd make you carry me."

I laughed as she stood up straight and put some effort into her steps. Though she liked to call me short, I had no trouble keeping her pace. People assumed Sprites and Gnomes were the height of children at our tallest, but we actually averaged five-foot-three, and Maeve only towered over me because of her mixed heritage from somewhere generations ago. Besides, nothing was going to slow me down today.

I was finally going to start working on the project I've dreamed of ever since I arrived in Moonlit Falls. Three long years of proving my skills as a gardener to the town council, making every tree, flower, and shrubbery look their best, and bringing the natural beauty out of this small town. At last, they had relented and gave me permission to renovate the eyesore they tried to call green space in the northwest part of town. The large space was home to only a few things: trash, weeds, broken benches, and the most beautiful oak tree I had ever seen.

The ancient tree had to have been older than most of the town, and I immediately knew I couldn't stand by and let such a beauty be surrounded by the dilapidated land. I'd begged and pleaded with the council while I worked as the town gardener, but they had never let me do anything with the land beyond a little clean-up now and then. They called my ideas "too expensive", even with my cost-saving Earth-magic. But at long last, I got the final council vote I'd needed to put my plan into action. Today was the day I was finally going to dig in—literally.

We approached the site, a couple of streets in from the riverside, up the road from the sports center. This area of town was surrounded by small buildings, all grouped close together. It gave the area an older atmosphere compared to the nearby city. As we stepped onto the land, my eyes locked onto the bowed arms and ancient bark of my favorite part of Moonlit Falls.

Being an Earth-Sprite, I always felt a kind of magnetic pull to ancient trees. I found that the older the tree was, the more they liked to tell me their stories of days long past. Young buds were just as chatty as their veteran counterparts, but they preferred to dish out the town gossip instead of telling epic tales.

But for reasons I couldn't explain, this tree was almost silent. Though the branches overflowed with life and color, this old oak had only ever spoken one word to me. On the day we met, when I laid my hands on the gnarled bark, she whispered her name.

"Delwyth."

Maeve let out a low whistle as we stepped onto the patchy grass. "She sure is a beauty. I see why you come here almost daily. Her presence is... it's hard to describe. Soothing, maybe?"

I nodded. "It's like I can think clearly around her. She reminds me of Wales, and of the raw magic there. She feels like home."

"You mean you didn't decide to stay here just for my charming personality?"

"Stop pouting, you know I love you."

"I do, I just like to hear you say it. Now, remind me what you need me to do here?"

I looked around the open space with Delwyth in the center. It was a large area, just under a quarter acre, with the delicate skeletons of long-forgotten shrubs dotted around the perimeter. They were interspersed with plots I supposed once contained flower beds, but were now the tangled remains of dried weeds, the flowers long choked out of their home.

At least half a dozen wooden tables and benches sat rotting near the far side of the area, encircling a particularly bedraggled patch of grass. The grass lay flat and muddy from people's footprints, a result of mostly being used as a shortcut across the square rather than the beauty spot it was originally designed for.

Moonlit Falls wasn't what people would class as a rough town—far from it, actually. It was quaint, with cobblestone paths and narrow streets. I was most proud of introducing hanging baskets of flowers outside some of the shops down

Main Street, which I maintained weekly. They brought a closer sense of community within the town, and I had plans to add small lights around them for Christmas later in the year.

Yet this spacious area had been neglected time and time again by the town council, for no reason other than finances. Despite being in the center of town, this eyesore had been left to crumble into disrepair. It was easy to see that some semblance of planning had been used originally, before it was cast aside for the more urban projects in the town. Still, the bones of the land were good, and the potential for something better was there.

"I need you to work your magic with those weeds in the old planters and get anything dead off the land so I can start working the soil. I'll start getting rid of the benches."

Maeve nodded and cracked her knuckles. Gnome magic was perfect for this, they had an affinity for not only tree roots, but all plants. Maeve would be able to sense even the smallest stragglers and raise them above ground to be dealt with.

"Easy, I can do that. Tricky thing will be avoiding Delwyth's roots. I can feel them running all over the place—pretty deep, too—but I'll be careful." Maeve waved her hand at me to relax and headed for one of the old flower beds to get started.

I took a deep breath and curled my toes in the damp soil. It was time to get started. I could hear the town starting to wake up around me; people were bustling on their way to work or school. I imagined the queue at Jewels Cafe was probably already out the door by now. I made a mental note to stop by for a coffee pick-me-up later, once I'd earned it.

I picked up a piece of the first bench and was surprised by its lightness. It was honestly a good thing the land looked as bad as it did. If someone sat on these things, they'd break instantly. I started splitting the remnants of the bench into two piles: one of wood and one of metal fixings. I could feel the sweat starting to run down my spine, between my wings.

"Eww, eww, nope! No, that's too gross." I frantically dabbed the lower part of my shirt against my back to catch the little rivulet of sweat making a mad dash for my ass. I jumped when I heard a deep voice from behind me.

"Wow, I really hope you aren't talking about me."

Spinning around, I tried to make it look like my hand wasn't awkwardly racing the sweat to my asscrack. "Erich! H-How long have you been standing there?"

Holding back a laugh, Erich smiled, and my heart melted. That smile could charm the panties off a nun, and any god would agree it was the right decision. He wasn't a tall man by local standards. With all the supernatural genetics in this town, the average height for a man was at least six feet. Erich was somewhere around five foot six, but with his strong body and enamoring smile, Erich was a fantasy for the majority of girls, gays, and theys in Moonlit Falls.

"Long enough to see you wipe the sweat from your butt. Y'know, if you had a back to your shirt, you'd probably catch that faster," he replied with a smirk.

I laughed at his gentle tease and sighed a little to myself. He was right, of course, but all my shirts were low-cut at the back to allow space for my wings. Wings that Erich couldn't see because of the town's cloaking wards, keeping supernaturals hidden from humans.

I've never been sure what humans see in place of the magic in this town. We had a similar spell back home, in Wales, where the spell made the humans' brain replace the magic with something that made logical sense. Like how your brain erases your nose from your everyday vision, instead of it being in the center of everything you see. It's there, it's just not visible.

Erich had probably seen me do magic hundreds of times over the few years I've known him. We've had full conversations while I hovered by the hanging baskets. My best guess is that he imagined he saw me on a ladder. He'd never know about my wings unless I outright said to him, "Hey, look at me flying!" Which wasn't something I could do.

It was almost sad that he never saw the magic of this town, but there were rules around humans and magic. Mainly that they don't mix. There have been a few humans who have known the secret, and things have remained safe, but the cloaking wards exist to protect supernaturals. Hunters have caused too many supernatural deaths, and towns like Moonlit Falls have remained as a haven to those more vulnerable.

As much as I'd love to show Erich what I am, there have always been too many risks.

"Anyway, I thought I'd drop by on your big day! Finally doing something with the old Village Green park, huh?"

"Is that what this used to be? I thought this was where nature's dreams went to make bad decisions," I deadpanned.

"You're not wrong there. But you've been talking about this project for months, so I wanted to give you something to commemorate the special occasion." Erich reached into his back pocket and pulled out a long piece of fabric. It was printed with leaves in gorgeous shades of burned reds and yellows. "You always wear your hair back with headbands while you work, I thought this one would look great in your collection."

I held in a squeal of delight and hugged him tightly. "Thank you, thank you! It's so pretty!" I felt his arms wrap around me as he chuckled at my reaction. I quickly pulled away as I remembered how sweaty I was. "No, wait, I'm gross!"

"You're not gross, you're just... I was gonna say 'moist', but that's worse, isn't it?"

"Much worse. But thank you. I love the headband." I untied the current band that was keeping my strawberry-blonde hair out of my face and replaced it with Erich's fall leaves.

"Looking good, Flower-Girl." Erich grinned, obviously pleased with himself, then looked down to his watch. "Ah, I gotta go. Deliveries aren't gonna drive themselves. But I'll stop by tomorrow, cool?"

I grinned. "Yep! I should have most of this removed by then."

"Perfect. Good luck!" Erich jogged over to his van parked at the post office across the street. I'd be lying if I said my eyes didn't wander down to watch his fantastic ass in those cargo shorts.

Watching his van drive off into the town, I felt Maeve's arm slump around my shoulders. "So, are you done flirting now? I know that man looks like he was personally designed by a cupid, but I'm not here to drag dead plants out the ground while you drool over him."

"Huh?" I snapped out of my stupor. "Did I really drool?"

Maeve let out a small laugh as she wiped over my chin with her thumb. "Nah, you're clean this time. This headband is pretty cute, though."

"Yep. He knows just what I like."

"And yet you still insist you're just friends."

"We are!" I ducked out from under her arm and picked up another piece of broken bench to busy my hands. "We're totally just friends. I even called him 'buddy' last week."

Maeve cringed. "Oh, that one stings. Poor guy."

I let out a tired sigh. Erich had looked like he wanted to go jump off the top of the Falls when I said that to him. He deserved so much more than the Friend-Zone, but I couldn't offer him any more than that.

"I know it was mean, but it's not like I had much choice! I already risk too much just hanging out with him." I threw the piece I was holding onto the pile of wooden scraps and let out an exasperated groan. "Ugh, I just like him so damn much! He's thoughtful, and he gets me, and we have fun together. But I couldn't be with him without him knowing everything. It sucks!"

"Aggs, tell me what you need from me. Do you want the supportive best friend who tells you that love conquers all and you should go get some dick? Or do you want the friend who helps you convince him you're into girls?"

"I regret telling you so many things growing up."

"Yep, I still remember it all. Especially your ex-girlfriends." Maeve opened her arms and waved her hands at me. "C'mere, sweaty-girl. You need a cuddle."

"You're just as sweaty as I am. And it's called a *cwtch*."

"Hush, my little Welshcake. Just enjoy the disgusting mingling of our sweat in the least fun way possible." She rested her cheek against the top of my head as I held onto my bestie. "You're doing the right thing, Aggy, but you can still enjoy the friendship. He'll get over it, and if he doesn't... Well, we both know how to dig a really deep hole."

I snorted. "You're so right. Come on, I wanna get at least half this crap moved off the land today."

We pulled away from the embrace, and I inwardly groaned. This was going to be a lot more work than I expected.

CHAPTER TWO

THE LATE AFTERNOON SUN WAS STILL GOING STRONG AS I began packing up for the day. I was starting to feel that the sign I'd put up for the renovations to advertise my business, "Soil Sprite Gardening & Landscaping", was mocking me with its bright colors and cheery font.

I was exhausted, both physically and mentally, as I balanced the new Village Green project with my daily gardening duties around the town. It was my fourth day on the site, and I was having a hard time admitting that things were progressing slower than I'd planned.

So far, we'd managed to get rid of the dried out bushes and weeds, and the pieces of benches had been picked up by the town council's recycling team; but we'd discovered a lot of large old stone slabs under the dirt, going across the northern side of the land. Our best guess was that the last people who tried to make this place look presentable had just laid turf over them instead of bothering to remove them properly.

Moving the slabs, even with magical assistance, had taken most of yesterday. Today was finally spent adding new fertilizer to the exposed soil and giving it a magical boost to get the nutrients properly absorbed, but it was slow going without Maeve around to help. She only worked with me part-time while she finished her online degree in business, which we would need if we were ever going to be able to do more big jobs like this in the future.

As I packed away the last empty bag of fertilizer, I heard the song "Baby Got Back" blast from my back pocket. "Damn it, when did she change it again?"

Maeve had an annoying habit of regularly changing my ringtone when I wasn't looking. I really needed to change my passcode, but it kept slipping my mind. I pulled the phone from my pocket and felt a chill go down my spine as a photo of my mother's smiling face lit up on the screen.

She looked a lot like I did; we shared the same strawberry blonde hair and pale, freckled skin, but her eyes had a toughness that only came with experience of the world that mine lacked.

"Oh no. No, no, no..."

My mother was generally nice enough as a person, but conversations with her could be difficult and had been ending in arguments lately. She loved telling me all about the gossip back home in an effort to coerce me back, ignoring the fact that I've been happy in Moonlit Falls the whole time I've been here. But it looked like it was time to go another round.

I took a few deep breaths while that damn song continued to blare out. I paced in a small circle before settling at the base of Delwyth's large trunk. If I had to have another one of these calls, I'd at least do it somewhere I felt safe.

I clicked 'accept' on the call and brought the phone to my ear, "Hiya, *Mam*. You all right?"

Her voice immediately boomed through the small speaker, ignoring my question completely. "You will not believe what the neighbor of your cousin's brother-in-law has done this time."

I immediately felt my eyes start to roll back in my head, and I held in an exasperated sigh. "*Mam*, you know I have no idea who you're on about."

"You know, the one who had that house fire by burning rubbish in the wheelie bin too close to the shed."

"Oh, yeah, Lewis." I shook my head. I really didn't have time for this. "Look, I'm just finishing up work at the minute. Can this wait a bit?"

I regretted those words the moment they left my mouth.

"Really? Again, Agate? Seems like all you do is work. What's today's task, weeding a lawn?" I know she meant that to be insulting, but in reality she wasn't far off the truth.

"Actually, this week I finally started on the Village Green renovation site I've been talking about."

"The one with the oak tree?"

"Delwyth, yeah."

"Still haven't got any more words out of that lump of bark yet?"

"*Mam*, she's more than that!"

I heard her deep sigh down the phone. "If all you've managed to get out of that tree is a name, its time has come. It's as good as gone, Agate."

I looked up at Delwyth from where I sat. Her leaves shone a bright green in the afternoon sunlight, and even though her bark was rough and mottled, I could feel a strong pulse of life at the core.

"No, you're wrong. Delwyth has *so much* life inside her. I just know that if I can heal the land around her, she'll be able to really speak to me."

"And then what? Even if you're right, what do you really think this project is going to prove? Agate, please. You always seem to make time for trees, but you never make time for family anymore. You know how hard it's been on me, you moving all the way over there."

I groaned at her attempt at guilting me. "I know, I'm sorry for that. But I love this town, and this'll prove I can do some good here! I feel something here that I never felt back home. You always said to follow my feelings."

"But you should be here!" she snapped at me, then paused as her tone softened. "You've always been such a sensitive soul. You're not made for going off on your own."

"I'm doing well here, *Mam*. Maybe being a 'sensitive soul' is *exactly* why I should be here!" I threw her words back at her. "If you visited, you'd understand what I'm talking about."

"You need to stop acting like a stubborn child and come home." That comment stung hard enough to bring tears to my eyes. "Your brother and your cousins have all fit into their roles here wonderfully, it's what you always wanted growing up."

"Tending to the Fae Woods isn't what I'm meant to do with myself. I've made a life here, I have friends here." I tried to speak steadily, with confidence, but my voice wavered. "I made my choice, and I'm going to see it through."

There was silence for a moment before she spoke again. "Okay. You've clearly made your bed. Just be cautious."

The line went dead without a goodbye, and I stared at my phone screen. I couldn't believe what my mother had said to me. We didn't always see eye to eye, even now with me being an adult, but to know she thought so little of me? I put my phone back in my pocket, looking instead at Delwyth.

I wasn't going to be made to feel like a silly child for believing there was more to this ancient oak tree. The large, twisting limbs towered over me, surrounded by summer green leaves. But beneath the beauty of Delwyth, that strange, pulsing energy remained. An energy that called to me.

I'd chosen to travel all the way to Moonlit Falls a little over three years ago, but I was still just a little girl to my mother. To her, I was still the wide-eyed child who needed to be saved from trying to sneak up on the Kelpies and flying after the Salamanders.

"What do you really think this project is going to prove?"

I had to force myself to stop replaying my mother's stinging words in my head while tears burned down my cheeks. As I took a deep breath in through my nose, the scent of the damp soil filled my lungs and squished between my exposed toes. I took another breath and focused my mind on those routine sensations; the dirt digging beneath my nails and the rough tree bark against the palm of my hand, the gentle breeze on my gossamer wings, making them sway lightly.

"I can do this." I choked the words out against the lump in my throat. My eyes ached as I fought back against the tears threatening to consume my spirit. I rose up to my full height, refusing to cower any longer at the thoughts of what could go wrong. I had to at least try. I owed myself that much.

I took a step forward, my always-bare feet moving tenderly across the terrain, and as my weight shifted to that foot, I felt the ground rumble deep inside the Earth.

Birds shot out of the upper branches into the sky as

Delwyth let out a deafening groan of pain. My knees shook as I desperately tried to stay upright, frantically looking for any passersby around to help. Anyone at all, until... silence.

I slowly backed away from Delwyth as my eyes scanned the area in front of me. The last few leaves shaken from their homes above me gently glided to the ground. My heaving breaths were the only sounds left in my ears. The ground sat still, as though nothing had happened. Delwyth was a little more bare than she had been a few minutes ago, but otherwise, she appeared as peaceful as normal.

So what the actual fuck just happened here?

That question circled my mind until my foot met something thick, damp, and weirdly spongey on the ground. My body stilled. That definitely wasn't soil.

I barely had the time to look down before the thing under my foot was wrapped around my ankle and squeezing firmly. My bottom hit the ground with a thump. I let out a surprised yell, and my wings flapped rapidly, attempting to pull my leg away to safety. Instead, I was pulled closer to my captor. The binding wrapped farther up my leg, reaching my thigh. A mouth filled with needle-sharp teeth opened in front of my face and hissed furiously.

I froze as I met the golden-brown eyes of a snake. It was difficult to tell with it wrapped around my leg and its face too close to my own for comfort, but it was easily double my body length and thicker than my arm. I was no expert, but at that moment, I was willing to bet it was the kind of snake that loved a delicious little Sprite as a late-afternoon snack.

Its large head tilted curiously as it met my terrified stare, slowly closing its jaw filled with far too many teeth for my liking. Its forked tongue flicked out against my cheek while its gaze gradually traversed my body, my right leg still encased in its thick, scaled form. I carefully leaned my upper body as far away from the literal jaws of probable death as I could.

"Nice snakey... Good snakey..." my voice squeaked out. "You can let go whenever you want. A-Anytime now really would be great, please."

Its grip loosened slightly on my leg, and I shuddered out a small breath of relief. Faster than I could blink, it lunged in again aiming straight for my neck. I fell, my back hitting the ground hard, crushing my wings, and I braced for the pain. Instead, a deep chuckle met my ears, and I tentatively opened my eyes.

"Gotcha."

Above me sat a pale man with a grin rivaling the Cheshire Cat. His dark hair flopped over his forehead, drawing my eyes to his high cheekbones and pointed nose. Amber irises with their slitted pupils remained, proving to me that the man and the snake were one in the same. A shifter.

I ground my teeth. Infuriated by his smug grin, I shoved my hands against his chest. "What the *hell* do you think you're playing at?!"

"Me?" Shock glossed over his features as he pulled my right leg up by the ankle. "I should ask you the same. It's really not polite to step on people when they fall out of a tree y'know. And with dirty, bare feet no less. You got something against shoes?" His reptilian eyes scanned over my muddy foot, his lips sneering in disgust.

I yanked my leg back out of his grip, delivering a swift kick to his ribs. He faltered with a small gasp, a muddy stain now smearing his charcoal t-shirt. I mentally high-fived myself for my little victory and sat up on my elbows, shuffling back a few steps.

"I didn't mean to step on you, but that was no reason to attack me!"

He didn't look up at me from picking the larger clumps of dirt off his shirt. "Attack you? Oh, Tinkerbell, if I'd really attacked you, we wouldn't be talking now. And I'm still waiting for your apology for knocking me from the tree."

I paused in my retreat. "That... that wasn't me."

He raised an eyebrow, finally meeting my gaze again. "Well, who else could it have been? I can smell that you're Fae. I'm guessing a Sprite? Or some kind of Faerie. I've seen you working here all day. Your magic hit that old bastard of a tree just now and threw me off the branches mid-nap. Hell of a way to wake up."

He stood up and cracked his neck. "But I guess I can forgive you. I did get to scare you pretty good." He sniggered to himself at the memory and lowered his hand in a silent offer to help me up. "I'm Marcus."

I took in his relaxed form and narrowed my eyes at his hand. My wings fluttered behind me and raised me up until my pointed toes barely brushed the Earth. I turned away from him, silently enjoying how he awkwardly retracted his hand, and I glided over to Delwyth. I dug my feet in the soil, placed both of my hands on her gnarled bark, and breathed deeply. My magic never usually acted up the way Marcus claimed, but that didn't mean it was impossible. I had been feeling some pretty intense emotions at the time, so he could be on to something.

"Byddwch yn ddiogel ac yn gryf Delwyth." Be safe and strong. I whispered the prayer in *yr Hen laith*, the Old Language, and gently placed a kiss to seal the spell.

"So usually people respond with their name when someone introduces themself. Or do you just prefer trees that don't talk back?"

As I turned back around, Marcus watched me carefully with those unnerving snake-eyes. "My name is Aggy."

"Aggy? I'll assume that's a nickname. What's your full name? Agatha?" He grinned at his own joke as I stayed quiet, leveling a sharp glare at him.

"What do you want, Snake-boy?"

"Ooh, so she does have a little bit of sass stored away in there. I'm a python, by the way. It's important to be specific or the cobras will get bitchy with me again." He rolled his eyes and shrugged his shoulders, then slowly started walking towards me. I took a step away and felt my back bump against Delwyth's trunk. "All I wanted was an afternoon nap somewhere warm, plain and simple. I thought it'd be quiet here, since no one seems to come to this part of town. Well, except for you, apparently."

Marcus stopped within arm's reach of me and looked me up and down, his eyes focusing on mine. It was as if he was looking at more than my face, but I couldn't decide if it was creepy or somehow enthralling. Like his eyes were daring me to meet them and let him see everything about me.

I felt my cheeks heat and forced myself to look away from him. "Yeah, I work here. Hopefully, this renovation is gonna bring more people to this area. So, sorry for ruining your nap spot."

He shrugged, his eyes not leaving my face. "It's cool. I haven't been in town all that long, so I didn't really have any claim to it."

"You're just visiting then?" I don't know why I was suddenly interested in this man, but now that the scare had worn off, I could at least admit to myself that he was attractive. I was desperately trying to not look up at his smug face, but my eyes had other ideas. They liked that smug face a lot.

"Aww, don't look so worried. I'm sticking around." Turns out he was just as egotistical as he was attractive. The worst combination. "I'm looking for a place to move in with a friend. We have some old friends here who we're staying with for now, and we've decided we like this town."

"It's a great town. If you decide to stop letting your fangs get friendly with the space in front of people's faces, I'm sure you'll fit right in here."

That made him laugh, a deep chuckle that did something to warm my insides.

"You may have a point there." He nodded. "Well, Agatha, it's certainly been an experience. I'll leave you to finish off your tree-hugging for now, and maybe I'll come see you again sometime. Bonus points if you decide to scrub those toes between now and then." He gave me a wink and swaggered away from me with a lazy wave over one shoulder.

I scoffed at his comment and shouted after him. "Well, just don't scare any more of the locals, you dumb Danger-Noodle!" Not my best comeback.

He barked out a laugh as he turned the corner and headed farther into town, leaving me alone again at last.

"What a weird guy," I muttered to myself, then felt my shoulders droop and my jaw unclench as I finally allowed myself to relax.

I pulled out my phone and fired off a quick text to Maeve, asking what her preferred takeout for tonight was. After that awful phone call with my mother, and the encounter with Marcus that left my knees shakier than I was willing to admit, I was desperate for a girls night in.

CHAPTER THREE

I SWIFTLY RECEIVED TEXT ORDERS FROM MAEVE TO swing by Aphrodite's Pizza to pick up dinner and hurry home with the food. Aphrodite's was always quick to serve up the food, but they seemed especially fast to get my order ready today. Maybe Wren, the part-timer at the counter, could see the lingering mental exhaustion in my eyes from the phone call with my mother and took pity on me.

"Here you go, Aggy. One large veggie-supreme with extra chillies, one large Margherita with half the usual cheese, plus sides of garlic bread, mozzarella dippers, and onion rings." Wren smiled at me as she passed the boxes to me over the counter. The order never changed, but she always liked to check with me in case I decided to sway from the pizza routine and try something new. So far, no luck.

"Thanks, Wren. Say hi to Saffron for me. I keep missing her here lately."

"Yeah, she's on reduced hours for an internship at the moment, but I'll pass it on. See you again soon!" She gave me a little wave as I left with my boxes.

I flew home as the sun started to set over the horizon. The house Maeve and I shared was in the woods, past the north-west side of the town, along the Starlight River heading down from the Falls. It used to be part of a larger community of lesser Fae who wanted to be closer to the land while still being a part of Moonlit Falls. Most of the people who lived there had now moved into the town center or moved out to where the land called them.

The only neighbors we had left were Maeve's Gnome relatives, a few families of Brownies, a lone Banshee, some Will-o'-the-wisps, a group of Sylphs, and a small coven of Druids. Though the Druids weren't Fae, they had been welcomed all the same, since they shared our desire to be close to the Earth and the elements.

The houses in this community were made by Dryads, who had long since moved on from the town. My understanding from Erich, when he delivered our mail, was that our homes appeared as basic wooden cabins to humans. In reality, our houses were made from the trees themselves, and were much larger on the inside. Our front door was carved directly into the bark of a huge maple tree, but when it opened, you could see the real home.

We had a small open-plan living room and kitchen, with a laundry room off to one side, and a decently sized bathroom. A staircase led down to Maeve's basement-bedroom, and another went upstairs to my room and a spare. We were lucky that the Dryads enjoyed modern amenities as much as we did. The house had been hooked up with wiring and indoor plumbing for years without any issues.

"I'm back!" I called out to Maeve as I hovered inside and nudged the front door shut with my hip. I put the takeout boxes on the kitchen countertop as Maeve came upstairs from her bedroom.

"Holy shit, you look filthier than usual. I'm almost impressed."

I looked down at myself and grimaced. I loved soil. It was a part of me and I felt stronger with it around me, but I was practically covered head to toe from my rough introduction to Marcus. It did explain why my food didn't take long, though. They really did want me out of the store.

"Ugh, long story. I'm gonna shower real quick. Keep my food warm in the oven?" Maeve nodded, and I flew to the bathroom to wash the dirt off my skin. Maeve liked to keep the house tidy, so I had to clean off as soon as I got home each day. Today was definitely a step up from my usual level of 'delightfully rustic', as Maeve would describe it.

I undressed quickly, throwing my work clothes into a pile in the corner, then ran some hot water in the sink and scrubbed the headband Erich gave me by hand. There wasn't much dirt on the headband itself, but I could feel it caked into my hair and smeared down my back, between my wings.

After a shower that was hot enough to make a salamander-shifter sweat, I grabbed my pizza from the oven and joined Maeve in our cosy living room filled with houseplants. Most were in pots along the window sills and walls, but a few hung in baskets from the ceiling, framing a wall of decorative Welsh lovespoons that I'd been collecting for years. They reminded me of home, while still being part of the woodsy-atmosphere of the house.

Maeve had plopped herself on the couch with her half-cheese pizza in her lap, already a few slices down. "Thanks for getting dinner, Aggy. I really didn't wanna cook tonight." She had a tired look in her eyes, the one she usually had when she'd been staring at a screen all day.

"Coursework going okay?" I asked as I picked up my first slice and inhaled the spicy aroma.

Maeve shrugged as she finished a bite. "I guess so. I'm just tired. One of my lecturers doesn't like where my final essay is going, and he keeps using the phrase, 'Please, pass'."

"What a cheeky twat!" I gasped.

"You're not wrong there." She nodded while she reached for two slices of garlic bread and sandwiched a small handful of onion rings between them.

"Do you need me to sort him out? Seriously, give me the address. I'll have vines blocking up all his pipes before he knows what hit him."

Maeve seemed to seriously consider my offer before shrugging. "I'll admit, the audacity of that jerk is getting to me; but it's okay. I'll get it all done. Can't leave you to struggle working alone. Speaking of, did something happen today? You look like someone purposely stepped on a ladybug." She took a big bite of her makeshift sandwich and looked at me with her unconventional-therapist-eyes, the ones that told me to spill my guts before she forced me.

"Well, I had a delightful conversation with my mother. I hate you for changing my ringtone again by the way." Maeve grinned to herself, probably giving herself a mental high-five. "Right before I got scared by a sexy python. You know, the usual."

Maeve's eyes widened as she swallowed her bite and put the rest of the sandwich down. "I'm getting the wine. Stay there and get ready to explain."

I loved Maeve. She always knew exactly what I needed. "Do you want the mother story first, or the snake?"

"The mother! Knowing her, that one left more of a wound on you." I waited for her to grab a bottle of merlot and pour it out for us both before continuing. I explained the conversation I'd had with her between bites of pizza, and I was honestly a bit proud of myself for not screaming it all out in one breath.

"Yikes. That sounds bad, even for her. Do you think she'd actually come visit, though?"

I shook my head. "Nope. I mean, she loves a holiday, but visiting me would be like admitting that this is my permanent home. As far as she's concerned, this is all some phase and I'll be back soon."

"But you've been here like three years, and you've only visited home for Yule once, two years ago." Maeve raised a dark eyebrow, silently asking me to confirm.

"Yup." I popped the 'p' and took a long sip of wine. "She loves to live in her own head, I guess."

"Crazy bitch. Sorry, I know she's your mom and all, but she's really fucked up on this one."

I grimaced, unable to deny it. "No, you're right. But it's so annoying because I know it's just her weird way of caring about me." I let out a long sigh. "I'm sure she'll call again once she's cooled off and act like the conversation never happened."

"What a healthy relationship you both share." We clinked our glasses together and drank to that. Maeve refilled them. "Now, tell me about the snake. Did you say it was a sexy snake? Uh, the fuck?"

"Python," I corrected her, reaching for the mozzarella dippers. "Apparently, it's an important distinction."

"My question remains, the *fuck*?"

I thought about how best to answer her as I chewed. "He was a shifter. Said that I knocked him from Delwyth's branches with my magic, but I dunno if that's actually true. Wasn't a conscious choice, that's for sure."

Maeve nodded in understanding and motioned for me to continue as she settled in for more storytime with wine. I quickly described my encounter with Marcus giving me the fright of my life, not wishing to relive that particular moment for too long.

"Wait, so you're just standing there talking to a naked snake shifter? Y'know with his, um, *snake*... hanging out?"

"No, he was clothed when he shifted back, thank the Goddess."

Maeve let out a low whistle. "Damn, you really were lucky then. I only know a few shifters powerful enough to shift with their clothes. Your guy must have been a strong one."

"He's not my guy!" I said that way too quickly to be innocent, and Maeve raised an eyebrow with a smirk curling up the side of her mouth.

"Did something else happen with this guy? You did use the word 'sexy' earlier."

"I hate your memory."

"Stop trying to change the subject and spill it already."

I shrank back in my seat with a pout. My wings flopped around my sides. Though they looked delicate, they were surprisingly tough and malleable. I was even able to sleep on my back without any problems.

"He had this presence to him. Like, it was more than the laid back attitude and the damn grin on his face. He got right up in my space and he had this intense look in his eyes. It should have been scary, but after the adrenaline wore off, it just... wasn't. He looked at me like he was studying me, but his words had this flirty undertone."

"He's a shifter who messed with you and was probably

trying to get a reaction out of you. I guarantee he was flirting with you."

"Why do you look so happy about this?"

"Because I think it's good for you to meet people who make you do that squirmy thing you're doing right now."

I immediately unfolded my legs and sat up straighter. Maeve was way too observant, and I needed to remember that if I wanted to keep hold of the last of my dignity around her.

"I don't want someone so arrogant, no matter how sharp their cheekbones are."

"Okay, that's a fair point. And I know Erich is basically the perfect, funny, supportive one for you, but it could be worth relaxing your expectations a bit. Be open to other possibilities. Like maybe a shifter with intense eyes?" I shot her a sharp glare. "Or maybe someone else. But I'm pretty sure you're destined for dick. You have that bisexual-disaster energy that dreams of a lady, but you'll end up with a guy. I'm calling it now, and I'll brag about this moment at your wedding."

"Of course you will." I sighed, knowing in my heart that she was right. "Fine. I'll consider more possibilities, but you have to as well! It's been nearly a year since you broke up with Ellis."

Maeve's eyes lit up with mischief. "You're right. Maybe I should give him a call on our break-up-iversary next month!"

"You wouldn't."

"You know I would. He was so much fun to make mistakes with." She broke into laughter at the end of her sentence and I joined her. Those two had been a disaster of a relationship when they were together, but they'd also been the life of the party. There had never been a dull moment when they were together.

As we finished eating, we started cleaning up the boxes and sorting the leftovers in the fridge. "So what's the plan for tomorrow? I can be free to help if you need it."

I thought for a moment. "I need to go to the school and do the rounds over there at some point. I can't put it off any longer. But could you do me a favor in the morning?"

"Hmm, ask the favor first, then I'll tell you if I'll do it."

"I need you to check on Delwyth. I couldn't sense anything wrong with her when I left today, but I need a second opinion. Marcus said I caused the tremor that threw him from the branches. What if he's right?"

Maeve's brow furrowed as she understood my concern. "Yeah, no problem. I don't usually sense things that you can't, but it won't hurt to check."

I pulled her into a tight embrace, relieved for her support, and felt her pat the top of my head. "Thank you. It's probably not going to turn up anything, but I'll feel better with a second opinion."

"It's okay, Welshcake. Now lemme go, I've got more work to do before bed." She pulled away and grabbed a bottle of water from the fridge, then headed towards the stairs down to her bedroom.

"Don't stay up late! It's gonna be another early start," I called after her.

"Ugh, no promises."

CHAPTER FOUR

I WAS EXTRA-GRATEFUL TO HAVE MAEVE WITH ME THE next morning to check over Delwyth. Something hadn't felt right since yesterday, and nerves had kept me awake most of the night. I looked rough, Maeve had kindly told me. So before we left, I'd spent an extra few seconds putting concealer under my eyes to try to hide the bags.

As we walked alongside the old church and headed into town, Maeve tapped my shoulder and pointed down the main street alongside the river. "Hey, why don't you go grab us some coffees and meet me at the site?"

I looked up at her. "Do I really look that tired?"

"Yep, you still look like hell. So maybe caffeine with extra sugar will perk you up a bit. Grab a muffin or something, too! Plus, it'll give me time to python-proof Delwyth before you arrive."

Did Gnomes have secret mind-reading abilities? I needed to look this up. Maeve always knew too much. I wouldn't admit it aloud, but I wasn't sure I was ready to handle another encounter with Marcus's beautiful, smug face without backup just yet. If I was able to avoid him while I was this tired, even better.

"You're the best, Maeve."

"I know, but it's good to hear every now and then."

We split at the end of the road in front of the church, and I started walking down Main Street. A wide variety of shops lined either side of the cobblestone road, giving the town a close-knit, cozy atmosphere. It had everything from a bakery to a water-based adventure store. Moonlit Falls was a great destination for both human and supernatural tourists.

I spotted Alexandrite unlocking the front door to Crafty Seductions and headed over to her. I'd been meaning to drop by for one of her pottery classes, but hadn't found the time yet. "Morning, Lex! Getting ready to open?"

She nodded, and a smile lit up her face. She had recently found her three mates and had started to settle down with them and their child. Things seemed to be going really well for her. Though I didn't know how she handled so many men in her life. It was impressive to balance that many people's emotions and needs.

"Oh! Hi, Aggy. Yeah, I'm running late this morning. Had to drop by the station and bail Tase out. Again. You'd think he'd be sneakier by now. Hey, you have a beautiful purple under your eyes this morning. Tired?"

I smiled at Lex's blunt honesty. "Mm, yeah. Yesterday was rough, and I didn't sleep well, but I'm waking up." I rubbed my cheeks and gave them a gentle slap. "See? Totally awake."

Lex raised an eyebrow, not convinced. "Unless you found yourself someone to ride, the way I've been on my guys, it's not a good thing to be looking that flat. What's up with you?"

"I'm fine, really! No, there was no, uh, riding for me, but I'm gonna go to Jewels and get some coffee before work. By the way, I should be around to check up on your flowers next week."

"Thank you so much! Seriously, they are so beautiful with you looking after them. Living things are not my strong suit. Except for Newt. You'll have to meet him sometime! Oh, and if you find someone to ride, I have this awesome book you can borrow for position ideas!"

I burst into laughter. Lex had an incredible way of caring about people's needs. All of their needs. "I'll let you know, promise!"

Lex gave me one of her signature smiles and headed into her store. "You better!"

I gave her a wave goodbye, then continued walking a bit farther up the street to Jewels Cafe. As normal for this time of the morning, they already had a queue out the door. I took my place at the back of the line, outside the large bay window on the front of the store.

I looked inside and smiled to myself. The interior of Jewels Cafe was beautiful with its multicolored glass lampshades hanging from the ceiling, showing exposed light bulbs and a stone fireplace in the center of the room. I was already excited at the thought of sitting next to that fireplace in the winter months. It looked like the perfect cozy spot.

I could see Nephrite, one of the owners, was serving Garnet, a local otter shifter and tour guide at Gaelach Teine. She was with one of her mates and co-workers, Bear, who was glaring at the cat tree in the corner, where Mocha was sitting in a loaf-position, completely content with himself. I guessed his irrational distaste for Mocha hadn't changed much. Bear kept his knees bent, as if he was ready to dodge an attack at any moment.

It looked like Garnet was trying to order coffee with her eyes and mouth still closed, just pointing at the chalkboard behind the counter and making shrugging motions. Poor Neph had a confused look on her face as she tried to translate what Garnet was trying to order in her semi-comatose state. Garnet was the furthest thing from an early bird anyone could get. I quickly learned to never try to talk to her before at least her second coffee.

Garnet finally received her coffee and impressively managed to navigate her way out, gently pulling Bear away from his feline nemesis by the sleeve, all with her eyes still closed. I made a mental note to remember not to complain about Maeve not waking up in the mornings. Compared to Garnet, she was a hyperactive toddler.

As the queue moved forward slightly, I hoped Neph and Bas were getting used to all the crazy local customers. Not that I had a right to talk. I'd made a deal with her when the store first opened: she'd let me come into the cafe barefoot if my feet didn't touch anything indoors. It was a fair deal, similar to how things were at home with Maeve, so I'd agreed quickly. I was able to walk barefoot on the outside decking, so that's where I preferred to sit and drink when I was eating in.

"Did I really just watch that guy give the 'I'm watching you' hands to a cat?"

I turned at the surprised voice behind me and found myself looking up at blue eyes so pale they could be gray. "Yeah, you haven't met Mocha?"

The stranger raised an eyebrow and flashed a smile. "I haven't, it's my first time here. Should I be worried?"

"Depends. Some of the other locals are suspicious of the poor thing. But he's harmless enough if you treat him right."

"Harmless *enough*?" he scoffed, clearly growing more suspicious of Mocha by the second.

I grinned at his reaction. "Scratch behind his ears when you see him wandering around town and you'll be fast friends, I promise."

"Okay. Good advice, uh…?"

"Aggy. Well, Agate, but everyone calls me Aggy."

"That's a cute name. I'm Nathaniel, but please call me Nate." He offered a hand for me to shake, and I took it. "Did this just become weirdly formal?"

That made me snort through a laugh as we moved up in the queue next to the door. "It did, but everything is a bit weird in this town. Haven't seen you before, though. You're new here?"

Nate gave me a short nod, making his dark blonde hair bob around his head. It looked like it was growing out of a cut. He could probably tie it back if he tried. Definitely the kind of hair you could run your hands through.

"A few days. I'm helping out Bailey and Ellis at the magic shop down the street. I never knew so many supes lived here, but apparently it's great for business. Good enough to call in an extra witch, anyway."

He was a witch! That made things a lot easier than trying to avoid supernatural-talk. "Yeah, they've been really popular since they opened. I go in a lot for spelled fertilizer and tools. Makes my gardening work way easier on big jobs."

"You're a gardener?"

"Perfect job for an Earth Sprite, don'tcha think?" I fluttered my wings slightly for emphasis before beginning my hover as we finally made our way inside Jewels Cafe.

"It sure fits. So, what do you recommend getting here? I've got a list for the guys but no clue what to get for myself."

Unlike with my repetitive pizza order, I had actually been determined to work my way through the entire Jewels Cafe menu. I'd heard that someone in the original store had done it, then started combining ingredients to make her own weird drinks. I wasn't planning on going that far, but I liked having lots of options with my caffeine, and so far, Jewels hadn't disappointed.

"Okay, so if you're looking to relax, you wanna get a Mood Tea. If you want to relax with sugar, whipped cream, and sprinkles, you want a unicorn hot chocolate. Then there's the coffee selection. You've got your basics in there, sure, but the really good stuff is on the specials menu. I haven't tried them all yet, but if you're unsure where to start, you should always go for the specials."

"You've thought a lot about this, haven't you?"

"It may not seem like it, but I just held back a lot."

Nate and I shared a laugh at that. He was so easy to talk to, like Erich, but with this quiet confidence in himself. Not arrogant like that jerk from the other day, though.

"Alright, Miss Aggy, since you're the expert, why don't you order my first Jewels Cafe coffee for me? Then as a thank you, I could take you out tonight."

"T-Tonight?" My brain was having trouble catching up with how fast this guy made a move. In my head, the hamster had finally started running on the wheel and then tripped over his own feet and started spinning out of control before landing on his cute little butt. An unhelpful reaction when a handsome man was waiting for an actual answer.

"Yeah, if you're free and you want to, obviously. No pressure. You just seem like a fun person to get to know around here." He shrugged one shoulder, and I wondered if my surprised response had embarrassed him or knocked his confidence. Why wasn't that damn hamster back on the wheel yet?!

I opened my mouth to answer him, but was quickly interrupted by Nephrite's perky voice. "Morning, Aggy! What can I get for you today?"

I held up a finger to Nate with a smile. "Hold that thought?" He nodded, and I turned back to Nephrite. "Morning, chick. Can I get a mint chocolate latte with an extra shot of espresso, a caramel macchiato with a rainbow swirl, and a white chocolate mocha to go?" I heard a small meow from the cat tree as Mocha heard his name, almost like he was approving the order.

Nate leaned down a little and spoke in a low voice near my ear. "Dare I ask which of those I'll be drinking? They sound good, though."

My cheeks flushed, but I focused my eyes on Neph working haphazardly behind the counter. She looked like she was chatting to the espresso machine while pulling levers. "It's a surprise, and I think you'll like it."

"I think you're right." He stood up straighter and quickly checked his coffee list, then spoke to Neph. "Can I add two hazelnut lattes and a mocha frappuccino to that order, please? I'll be paying for it all."

Nephrite gave him a slightly crazed nod as she made up the drinks.

I looked up at him. "You don't have to do that."

He grinned at me. "Oh, I'm not. Bailey and Ellis are paying. This is definitely a work expense."

I laughed and couldn't wait to tell Maeve that her mocha was just paid for by her ex. She was going to love that.

"Well then in that case, I'll just go pay my respects to the king over there for a moment." I glided over to Mocha—who was still in loaf-mode—and gave him some ear-scratchies. His purr rumbled loudly, and I booped his nose before heading back to the counter where Bas—the other cafe owner and one of Neph's mates—had handed over all the drinks in their takeout cups with printed jewels on the side to Nate.

I made sure he had the caramel macchiato I ordered for him as we headed back to the door. "You'll thank me later."

"At dinner, I hope?"

I landed gently on the ground outside Jewels and turned to look up at Nate again. He seemed earnest enough. Combined with a decent sense of humor and willingness to try new things, not to mention being a supe, he could be an interesting person to get to know.

"I can do dinner tomorrow night, is that okay?"

He flashed a smile at me, almost dazzling me a little. "Tomorrow works. We could meet here at seven and go get some food in town. I'll leave it to you to recommend somewhere."

"Sounds like a plan. I'll... um... I'll see you tomorrow then."

He headed to the front door of Moonlit Magicks and nodded. "Tomorrow, Aggy!" He raised his cup to me, then headed inside.

I had to hold myself back from skipping back to the Village Green. Maeve was going to be so proud of me!

I made it over to the site quickly and found Maeve kneeling at Delwyth's base. She had one hand on Delwyth's trunk and another on one of her large roots. Maeve's eyes were closed in deep concentration, and she looked like she was muttering a spell under her breath.

She opened her eyes and stood up straight once I reached her.

"Anything?"

Maeve bit her lip on one side, something she usually only did when she was nervous. "Something isn't right, but I don't know what. It's more likely a reaction to the fresh soil surrounding her. She's probably not used to having actual nutrients. But I think we should keep an eye on her."

I breathed a sigh of relief. It wasn't the best news, but at least I wasn't the only one who sensed something was off. "Good idea. We'll leave her for now to acclimatize and see how she is on Monday. I might pop by over the weekend just to check on her, but I won't work on the site."

Maeve nodded and took her coffee from the cardboard holder. "Hey, what's that on your cup?"

"Hm?" I looked down at my coffee cup and found a string of numbers scrawled along the side next to a letter 'N'. "Oh! Must have been Nate."

"Nate? Who's Nate? Why haven't I heard of Nate?"

I backed up a few steps from Maeve's frantic questioning, holding back a laugh. "I met Nate at Jewels, just now. We're going for dinner tomorrow night."

There was a long pause as she processed the information before letting out a high-pitched squeal. "Yes! I'm so proud of you, Aggy!"

CHAPTER FIVE

The rest of the day was spent catching up on my routine duties around town for the council. I'd been neglecting the other plants and trees around town while my focus was on the Village Green project this week, so I ended up working later than usual while I hurried to catch up. The new project was taking up so much of my time the past week, but I knew it would all be worth it soon.

I had finally given up for the day after my fingers got covered in cuts from a particularly nasty rosebush. I had been getting careless in my rush, and it wasn't getting me anywhere.

Maeve suggested I take Saturday as a much-needed rest day before going to meet Nate and I agreed. I was starting to think she was more excited about the date than I was. She had been fussing over what I was going to wear all day. I hadn't told her that he was working with her ex, Ellis, at Moonlit Magicks yet. I didn't want her to worry if Nate was just like Ellis, so I decided I was going to wait and see if there was going to be a second date first.

I finally left the house and flew into town to meet Nate

with just enough time to walk slowly down Main Street to catch my breath from the flight. Maeve's insistence on curling my hair and doing my makeup had taken longer than we'd thought, but I had to admit she'd done an awesome job. With a light smokey eye, my fall leaves headband from Erich holding the loose curls hanging down my back, and a burgundy halter-top dress in my usual bohemian style, I looked like the local gardener had leveled up. I'd even put some thin sandals on my feet so we wouldn't get weird looks in a restaurant. I was nailing this dating thing already!

Nate was already waiting for me outside Jewels and smiled as I approached. I took a moment to appreciate the dark jeans and light shirt with the sleeves rolled up his forearms. Definitely a memory to hang on to.

"Hey, Aggy, you look amazing. That dress really suits you." He looked me up and down, and my wings did a little flutter of appreciation.

"Thanks, it has pockets!" Smooth, Aggy.

"So, where are we going tonight? After the coffee you chose for me, I'm probably gonna be relying on your expert recommendations for everything in this town now."

"You really liked it?"

He nodded with wide eyes, like he was still surprised by how much he actually enjoyed it. "I still don't know what the rainbow swirl is, but I might need it in every drink now."

"Perfect! Another person successfully converted to the rainbow swirl! My plan for world-coffee-domination continues as planned." I grinned to myself for a moment before trying to restore my composure, but I realized Nate was laughing with me. He actually liked it when I said the weird stuff in my head.

"So I thought we could go to Nessie's Pub tonight. The

food is so good, and there's a local band, Nightly Vamps, playing in an hour or so. They're an alternative rock band, but they're doing an acoustic set tonight, so it should be pretty chill."

"That sounds pretty much perfect. Shall we?" He offered his hand, and I took it without hesitation.

Nessie's Pub was around the corner from Jewels Cafe, opposite the wharf. A fireplace divided the inside into two sections; the seating and dining area, and the standing area with a small stage and dance floor. The band was setting up, so we headed to the side with tables and grabbed a seat.

Warren, the bartender, saw us sitting down and came over while the bar didn't have anyone waiting. "Aggy! Good to see you! Who's your friend?"

I smiled up at Warren. He looked intimidating. He was a shockingly tall minotaur with huge horns, but he was easily the nicest person I knew in town. "Hey, Warren. This is Nate. He's new in town."

He looked down at Nate with a grin and shook his hand firmly. "Nice to meet you, Nate. Already trying to snap up our gardener, huh? Treat her right, okay?"

"I, uh, yes?" Nate looked from Warren to me, confused by how the conversation had turned.

Warren let out a laugh at Nate's expression and turned back to me. "Drink, Aggy?"

"Granny Rosie cider, please."

"And for your date?"

Nate smiled, his cheeks starting to go a bit red. "I'm trusting you here, Aggy. Same for me, please, Warren."

Warren nodded his approval. "Good move. I'll come back with your drinks and get a food order when you're ready."

I picked up a menu and passed it over to Nate as he

watched Warren go. He turned back to me with a smile still on his handsome face. "I'm guessing he's a friend of yours?"

"Yep. I like to come here with my roommate, and Warren is usually working. We usually just end up sitting at the bar all night talking crap together."

"Cheaper than therapy."

"Cheers to that as soon as the drinks get here."

We turned our attention to the menus until Warren returned with two pints of my favorite apple cider. "Here you go! Do you know what you want to eat?"

I motioned for Nate to go first, and he looked up to Warren. "Can I get the fish and chips from the specials?" He still looked a little nervous around Warren, but I nodded my approval of always trying the specials. He seemed to relax a bit then.

"I'll have the veggie lasagne, Warren. With—"

"With a side of garlic bread," Warren interrupted with a grin. "I gotcha, Aggy, don't you worry. Food won't be long, and try to stick around for Nightly Vamps's set later. It's not often they do acoustics."

"Thanks, Warren!" I called out as Warren went back behind the bar, then turned to Nate, who looked like he was deep in thought. "What's up?"

"Okay, I've been trying to place your accent, and I know I'm probably wrong, so I'm just going to ask: where are you from, Aggy? How long have you lived here?"

I smiled. It was common in this town for people to mistake me for Irish or Scottish with my accent, so it was nice of him to just ask me instead of just assuming. "I'm from a little town in West Wales. Been here for three years now."

"I've never been to Wales, but you've probably heard that a lot, though."

I nodded through a laugh. "Yeah, I have. But you should visit. It's really beautiful there."

"What made you move here?"

I paused to think for a moment, taking a sip of my cider while I thought about my answer. "I needed the change. My roommate and I were pen-pals way before we started living together, and she convinced me to take a chance and move over here. Once I started up my gardening business, things started to feel really right. Like this is where I'm supposed to be. What about you? You said you're a witch at the magic shop, right?"

Nate nodded and took a sip of his drink. "Oh, wow, that's actually really strong."

I grinned almost wickedly. "It's the good stuff, I promise. Now stop dodging and tell me about you! The mysterious stranger schtick will only work on me for so long."

He snorted a laugh and took another drink. "Okay, okay! Yeah, I'm working with Bailey and Ellis because they needed another witch in the business to deal with all the customers like you who are making them popular."

I put a hand over my heart and gasped dramatically. "I did this? The horror! If only I'd known what my purchases would cause!"

"Sarcasm will get you everywhere with me." He gave me a wink, then continued. "We know each other from university, so Bailey called me and said he could use my skills. My magic is pretty unique, so it's in demand for stores like theirs."

"Unique? How? If you don't mind me asking."

Nate was silent for a few seconds before he spoke a simple sentence that stunned me to my core. "My power lies in blood magic."

"Blood magic?" I breathed the words out, almost in a whisper.

I had heard so many rumors about blood magic in the supernatural community. I knew some obviously weren't true; like they were descended from vampires or that they only gained their magic from bathing in the blood of virgins on full moons every month.

But some rumors were harder to be easily dismissed as paranoid ramblings. There had been so many stories over the years of lives lost to blood magic. Mainly because of its association with ritual summonings—especially high-level demon summonings. People said that blood magic took power from life itself, and through it, its users could achieve immense levels of power. Which, in turn, could achieve immense levels of destruction and pain.

I knew I had to get out of the pub quickly. It was too dangerous here. Had he only wanted to meet me for my Fae blood? Sure, it wasn't as powerful as Elf blood or the blood of a High Fae, but it definitely had more power than a human's. Was this all a trap?

My eyes flicked between the door of the pub and the bar, as I wondered which of them was closest. The dining area wasn't busy yet, so there was space to get away. If only I could get past him quickly.

"Aggy! You're breathing too fast. You need to slow down."

Nate's voice pierced through my panicked thoughts, and I realized I was shaking. I couldn't breathe properly. I needed to get some air but didn't know how I would get past him.

"Aggy, it's okay. It's okay, I promise I'm not going to hurt you." He gently took my hand in his, and my head whipped around to meet his eyes.

My heart broke at his expression. He had moved around to my side of the table and was kneeling next to my chair, holding my hand like it was something precious. In that moment, his eyes matched my own; they were terrified. Mine for my life, his for what he was seeing.

"Please, Aggy." He spoke softly, slowly coaxing me back from my panic. "Let me explain. I promise you're safe." His thumb rubbed over my knuckles and I focused on that sensation, gradually slowing my breathing down to normal. His touch was so soothing to me, despite my heart trying to pound its way out of my chest.

"Y-You're..."

He gave me a sad smile. "I'm not what you think." He gave me a moment before he asked again. "Is it okay if I explain it to you?"

I wasn't sure what to say. My breathing was normal, but my mind was still spinning. He hadn't tried anything weird, and I didn't feel like I was actually in any danger around him. Maybe he deserved the benefit of the doubt. I gave a slow nod.

"Okay. Let's get some water, though. I think I should have a clear head for this."

"I'll go to the bar and grab you some." He let go of my hand and walked over to Warren, returning a moment later with a bottle of water. I checked the seal and it was unopened; I was giving him a chance, but I was still being careful.

Nate sat back down opposite me, as Warren came over with our food. Perfect timing.

"Thanks, Warren!"

"You okay, Aggy? You look a little paler than usual."

I nodded. "I'm okay. Thanks for the food." I looked over at Nate once Warren had returned to the bar. His eyes still held their fear. "I mean it, I'm okay now. Explain it to me, I'll listen at least." I picked up a piece of garlic bread and dipped it in the top of my veggie lasagne. "While I eat, I mean. Just, um, be gentle dropping any more bombshells on me, okay?"

He smiled, clearly glad I was no longer on the edge of a panic attack. "Thank you." He took a long drink of his cider and relaxed a little in his seat. "Blood magic isn't like other magical specialties. It's incredibly rare; it only appears every few generations within certain witch families. The last witch in my family to have the gift was my great-grandmother. I never had the chance to meet her, but she left a lot of books I was able to study from."

"You're self taught?"

He nodded. "I taught myself how to cast spells with my power-type. The fundamental theories of witch-magic are basically the same no matter what the specialty is. I was able to learn those basics like any witch, but the tricky thing was making it work for my personal magic. Once that was figured out, the only limit is power capacity."

I felt a shiver go up my spine at the word 'power', despite the food finally warming my stomach. I took another sip of water and waited for Nate to continue. I had to at least hear him out.

"Blood magic users have one of the worst reputations in the magical community, as you know. Your reaction was pretty standard." He smiled, wordlessly telling me it was okay. "For the most part, that reputation is well-deserved. There have been blood witches who have committed disgusting acts of magical violence in the name of power. But that's not what blood magic was originally used for. Can I see one of your hands, please?"

I looked at my hands, they were still covered in small

cuts—now scabbed over—from yesterday's rush-work in the rosebush. "I'm putting a lot of faith in you right now." I leaned forwards and put my right hand in his.

"I know. I won't hurt you." Nate pressed his thumb and rubbed over each of the cuts, whispering a spell under his breath. I gasped as his touch stung me, then calmed as a wave of relief took over. The pain was over before I even knew it, and as I looked at my hand, I realized it was completely back to normal. All of the cuts were gone.

"I found in my great-grandmother's books that the origin of blood magic was for healing."

"That's incredible! I've never seen healing magic performed like that. I thought only vampires could heal that fast, but you did it with just a spell."

"I used the dried blood from your cuts to heal them. My magic works best on physical things, it's less good with illusions. But I can infuse this healing energy into potions and amulets better than any regular witch. Blood is a powerful, scary thing, but it can be used for more than hurting people. At least, that's what I try to show. The stigma of blood magic will always be around, but I'd like to think I've at least changed *your* mind."

I looked up at him. We had both long given up on eating anything. He had a determined look in his gray eyes, masking the fear I'd seen before. I could tell he was telling the truth. I felt it in my core. He wasn't planning to hurt me, and he definitely didn't want me to be afraid of him.

I held his hand across the table and gave it a gentle, reassuring squeeze. "I think you've at least convinced me not to cut this date short."

Nate breathed a sigh of relief and squeezed my hand back for a moment. "I'll take that much at least. Now I still have a chance to convince you I'm a decent guy."

"Just decent?"

"I don't want your expectations to be too high. Give me some wiggle room."

I couldn't hold back the snort of laughter that burst out of me. It was a welcome change from the full-blown panic I'd felt earlier. "That seems fair. Do you wanna take our drinks over to watch the band? I think I'm done eating if you are."

"That sounds great. Let me go settle the bill. It's the least I can do after making you look like a deer in the headlights." He gave my hand a final squeeze before going back over to the bar.

I leaned back in my chair and finished off my bottle of water before taking a long drink of my forgotten cider. This date was not going the way I'd planned, but I think I was okay with that.

CHAPTER SIX

I WAS BLOWN AWAY BY NIGHTLY VAMPS'S ACOUSTIC SET. Nate and I had started watching it standing on the edge of the dance floor. By their third song, "Fangs For The Memories", the energy had pulled us in to dance together. Nightly Vamps had an incredible way of enchanting the audience, even with just acoustics. By the time they reached their final song, "Love In Your Blood", I was as exhausted from dancing as I was high on the music and the feeling of Nate around me. Luckily for me, he looked to be in the same state.

We stumbled out of Nessie's Pub, hand in hand, giddy and more than a little sweaty together. The sun had set and the night air was refreshingly cool on my clammy skin. Nate pulled at the neck of his shirt a little, trying to get some air moving around his chest, and I couldn't stop my mind from wondering how he would look without it.

"You okay? You have a dazed look in your eyes. Something on my shirt?" Nate asked me, sounding genuinely concerned. If only he knew where my thoughts actually were.

"I'm good! Just daydreaming for a second. Hey, you wanna get ice cream? We kind of skipped eating most of our food earlier and I know a cute place nearby."

"Perfect, lead the way."

I set off down the street at a fast pace, pulling Nate along by his hand until he quickly caught up with his long legs. The streets were pretty busy at this time of night. Families were heading home after eating out, couples and friends were only just heading out for a night of fun, and most of the nocturnal residents were just starting their day. Well... night.

Across the street from the Village Green site was Honey Bee's Ice Cream Shop, run by Jade's sister, Bee. Maeve and I made a habit of visiting Honey Bee's after particularly long workdays, so we could unwind and relax together. The flavors sold here were incredible: Watermelon Grape, Honey Bee Mine, and my favorite, Peanut Crunch Swirl. They stayed open late all year, making it the perfect after-date dessert.

Nate waved at Bee standing behind the counter as I pulled him into the shop. "I actually know this place! Bailey brought us all here when we first arrived because he's obsessed with the Lick Me Licorice."

"It's a good choice, but it doesn't beat Peanut Crunch Swirl. Double scoop in a cone please, Bee!"

Bee laughed from behind the counter. "You got it, Aggy! And for you?" She looked over to Nate as she prepared my cone.

"Uh, what was the chocolate one I had last time?"

Bee thought for a moment, then pointed down at her ice creams. "Oh, the chocolate flavor I recommend most is the Sugar Rush. It's a chocolate cake batter ice cream with brownies, caramel, and chocolate chips, then topped with whipped cream."

"Yes, that was it! It was like pure diabetes on a cone. I'll take a double scoop, please."

Bee smiled sweetly. She took so much pride in her creative flavors and it showed in just how delicious they were. Business had been booming for her all summer. I couldn't wait to see what flavors she would think to create next. Hopefully, my renovation work across the street would bring more people to this part of town, so she would see an extra boom in business. I had a really good feeling that people were going to love getting an ice cream from here, then going across the street to sit on the grass, in the sun.

Once we were back outside the store with our ice creams in hand, Nate pointed across at the Village Green. "'Soil Sprite Gardening and Landscaping'." He quoted the sign I'd put up for advertising while we were working there. "Is that you?"

"Yep. This is my current project; my dream project, actually. I've always wanted to do a complete renovation and redesign of a public space, and I couldn't have asked for a better one than this. I know it doesn't look like much right now, but did you see the state of it this time last week?"

"Yeah, I think you must have started this the day after I got into town. Will you walk me through your plans?"

The smile I gave Nate was completely genuine. With everything that had been happening lately with my mother and my own lingering doubts, I needed someone to show a real interest in my work. Maeve was great at pep-talks, but she was my best friend. It was in her contract. It felt different with Nate, in a really good way.

"I'd love to. Do you know any spells to light the place up a little? The street lights around here aren't great."

"On it. Hold this for me?" Nate handed me his ice cream cone, then pulled his keys out of his pocket and flicked the cap off a tiny blade. It was small enough to be mistaken for a nail file, but it looked deadly sharp. "Perfect for blood magic on the go, right? I don't think you'd appreciate me pulling out a switchblade."

Nate gave me a wink and pricked the meat of his thumb against the blade. He let a few drops fall. They burst into shimmering light the moment they left his hand. They multiplied and spread out over the space, lighting up the area. They reminded me of Christmas lights. This space was going to look stunning in winter.

Nate wiped the wound with his other hand, quickly healing the small cut, then put the blade on his keychain back in his pocket. "Thank you for trusting me to do magic in front of you."

"I get it now. The magic is only as scary as the person wielding it."

"Are you saying I'm not scary? I can be terrifying if you aren't careful. Especially if you don't give me back my ice cream." He teased me, a grin growing steadily across his face.

I fluttered my wings and hovered above the ground while giving my own ice cream a long lick. "I mean, my ice cream is great, but I wonder what yours is like. And I wonder if you can catch me before I find out."

"You're a terrible tour guide."

Nate lunged forward, and I couldn't tell if he was reaching out to grab me or his ice cream. I quickly swerved away from him in mid-air, narrowly avoiding his outstretched hands, then started leading him through the site.

"This is going to be a stone pathway leading in, it'll be lined with flowers, but I haven't decided what kind yet." I dodged another attempt at grabbing the ice cream and licked my own again before leading him to one of the site's corners. "Over here will be a few swing sets, some for kids and some for adults. We also ordered a small climbing frame for kids that should be good to set up in a week."

I soared up over Nate's head around the border of the site towards the other side, laughing as he ran after me. "We're planting community fruit trees over here! Anyone will be able to come pick fruit off the trees. They'll be completely free. We're thinking mostly apples and pears, but I want to get a small lemon tree in here, too. What do you think? Ah!" I ducked under Nate's arms trying to get me in a bear-hug, almost dropping the ice creams in my surprise.

"I think you're not playing fair!" Nate huffed. "But I'll get you! And your ice cream too!"

"Not if I finish eating it first! Now, along this side we'll have benches and a few tables. A beaver shifter friend of mine has been carving them by hand and we're adding some enchantments for a little extra protection against the outdoor elements."

I dodged another attempt from the side and led Nate to a corner of the site. "Over here we'll have a gazebo. It'll be the perfect spot for hosting parties or just spending time with the people you care about. Kind of like what we're doing now, but with less manic grabbing. Hey!" Nate's hand brushed my hip as he nearly got me that time. "Ooh, close! But we're nearing the end of our tour now, and I can't resist this chocolatey goodness for much longer." I teased as I flew to the center of the site and lowered my feet to the ground next to Delwyth.

Nate rushed up to me, and I let him pick me up around the waist and hold me close. I had the ice creams out at my sides, careful not to drop them, before bringing Nate's up to his mouth. He licked around the cone, catching the stray drips that were about to coat my fingers.

My eyes met his, and I felt my cheeks heat. His face was so close to mine, I could feel his breath tickle me. My voice came out a little above a whisper. "And all of it surrounds this tree, Delwyth. She's the star of this whole show. She's stunning. I want people to see her and love her the way I do."

"I agree this tree is stunning, but it's not the star of the show. That's you, Agate. You're the star here."

"Thank you... That was a really cheesy line."

"Yeah, I know, you're right. But it's the truth."

I opened my mouth to respond, just as Nate lowered his mouth to mine. His lips were soft as he kissed me firmly, but he didn't push me to deepen it. He seemed restrained somehow. He only let me taste him just enough that I was left wanting more when he pulled away and released the grip he had on my waist.

I did my best not to stare at him open-mouthed like a goldfish, but I was left a little dazed. He gently plucked his ice cream out of my hand and took a bite out of the cone. "I was wrong, you're not the worst tour guide after all."

I burst into laughter, not even attempting to hold it back. "Thank you, I think. But I don't think I'll be giving just anyone that kind of tour."

"That's kind of a relief to hear. Come on, it's getting late. I'll walk you home."

I took his hand and walked alongside him. "Actually, my

house is out in the forest near the river, which I'm guessing is a little out of your way. So how about I walk *you* home instead?"

"Are you sure?"

"Yep, I'll be flying home, anyway, so it won't take me long. But I'll wait until you're safely inside before I leave, and I'll text you when I get home. "

"Thank you, Aggy. But if we're going to where I'm staying for now, we should turn around. We're going in completely the wrong direction."

We headed back through the town as we finished our ice creams together. Nate mentioned that he was staying with Bailey and Ellis while their other housemates were out of town for a few weeks. Even though there was a small apartment above Moonlit Magicks, they actually lived a few streets away in a large house.

As we strolled up Main Street, I noticed a couple with a toddler holding a balloon leaving Astra's Moonlit Diner. The toddler was being carried by her father, resting her head on his shoulder, barely staying awake. Her little fist was clinging onto the balloon ribbon until she relaxed and it slipped through her fingers.

The toddler was suddenly wide awake as her cries rang out down the street. I was off my feet before I even consciously thought about it. My wings beat furiously in the air as I shot up the street and above the diner, grabbing the balloon by the ribbon.

I lowered myself to the ground gently in front of the toddler and handed her the balloon. "Hey, it's okay. See?"

She grabbed onto it with a chubby little hand, and her teary eyes were replaced by an expression of pure wonder. "You thwoo!"

Her mother came around and stroked the toddler's hair

as she smiled at me. "Thank you for that. She would have cried all the way home. That was quite an impressive jump!"

I realised quickly that this family were humans. The wards must have made them see me do an incredible jump with the balloon a lot lower than it actually had been.

"No, Mommy! She thwoo! The thawy thwoo!"

That was odd. I didn't sense any magic from the child or her parents at all. I stretched out my wings and watched as the toddler's eyes lit up in delight. She could definitely see them, but I could swear she was human. She shouldn't have been able to see my wings.

The father holding the child chuckled. "I'm sorry. She's been obsessed with fairies lately."

"Say bye-bye to the nice lady now." The parents started walking down the street away from the diner with the toddler safely holding onto the balloon nice and tight.

"Buh-bye, thawy!"

This was wrong. Unless the child had some kind of supernatural gene locked away that I couldn't sense, there's no way she should have been able to see me fly. I looked at Nate a few feet away and asked him, "Did she just see me fly?"

Nate nodded, a confused expression on his face. "I think so. But I didn't sense magic from her or the parents."

"Me neither. Am I overthinking this?"

He shrugged his shoulders. "Possibly, but it seemed strange to me too. Maybe the kid is just an anomaly?"

"Could be. She's so young, it's hard to say exactly what she saw."

We continued walking steadily through town, weaving through the side streets, until we were a few blocks away from the school in a residential area. The street was quiet except for the occasional passing car and other pedestrians.

It was strange. I still didn't know Nate very well, but I felt so comfortable being around him. Even though I'd been terrified of his magic in the pub, he managed to calm me just by being himself. There was something about him that put me at ease, but also intrigued me. That kiss had left me breathless in the best way, and there was a part of me that desperately wanted more.

Nate stopped outside a wide terraced house. It looked like it used to be two buildings that were combined into one. I looked up at him with my best flirtatious grin. "Is this the part where I kiss you goodnight on the doorstep and make sure you get home safe?"

"I won't say no to that."

Nate stepped forward and cupped my face in his hands before leaning down and kissing me tenderly. He still felt like he was holding something back from me, so I pushed up on my toes while pulling down on his shirt. He took the hint and wrapped an arm around my back, under my wings, pulling me up close to his chest. His mouth slanted across mine, and I felt his tongue lick at my bottom lip. I parted my lips to allow him access, but pulled my face away from him at the sound of a familiarly smug voice.

"Nathaniel St Clare! Are you making out with my favorite gardener on the doorstep without inviting me?"

I turned to see the face I was dreading. Marcus stood in the now open doorway, leaning on the hallway wall inside, wearing nothing but sweatpants and a shit-eating grin. Why did almost all shifters have a six-pack? Was it something in their genetics?

"What the hell are you doing here?" I asked.

"Me?" Marcus raised an eyebrow and pointed at

himself, before turning his finger to aim at me instead. "You're the one outside my house. Well, the house I'm staying in. Technicalities and all that."

My face whipped back up to Nate. He still had a firm grip, holding me close, which I was steadily starting to get mad about. "You live together?"

"Yeah, I had no idea you'd met. Marcus is my familiar." Nate explained it calmly, but I felt my heart drop to my stomach.

"Familiar?! But he's a shifter and you're..." I pulled my way out of Nate's arms as my eyes flicked between Nate's honest eyes and Marcus's amused ones, before my confidence crumbled. "I thought I asked you to be gentle with the bombshells!"

"In all fairness, I didn't really think this was a bombshell," Nate reasoned.

"Oh, it's a bombshell all right!"

"Now, Agatha, there's a great explanation for how I ended up becoming a familiar to this strapping man here. Nice to see you've invested in footwear, by the way." Marcus stepped forward casually, but stopped abruptly as I pointed a finger straight at his face.

"Not a word from you!"

This wasn't happening. I mean, it obviously was, but surely I wasn't actually deserving of this level of karmic bullshit.

I took a deep breath and a few steps away from the two men.

"Aggy—"

"Agatha—"

"No," I interrupted them both firmly, using a confidence I didn't know I had. "This was a really great night, Nate. But I'm gonna go home now and really think about... everything."

I turned to walk away, flexing my wings for a takeoff, but Nate's voice stopped me. "Agate, wait!" I glanced back at his conflicted expression, like he was fighting himself from running over to stop me from leaving. "Just... text me when you're home safe, okay? You don't have to say more than that. Just let me know you're safe."

I nodded once before beating my wings sharply and soaring above the houses.

CHAPTER SEVEN

"Agate, you can't spend another day in bed. I gave you yesterday as a freebie, but you need to work today."

I groaned beneath my duvet and snuggled in closer to my nest of pillows. I only left my warm cocoon for food and the bathroom yesterday, but it was Monday now, and deep down I knew that Maeve was right. I couldn't keep sulking about the disastrous end to my date the other night when I had things to do. That didn't mean I was happy about it, though.

"Actually, as the boss, I set my own work hours. And I say that this hour is for doing my best impression of a burrito."

"Uh-huh. And the hour after this one?"

"That's for reviewing the previous hour's work and making any improvements deemed necessary by the board of directors."

"There's a board of directors now?"

I reached my hand out of my duvet and pointed at the stuffed animals on the shelf across the room. "They're tough to impress and demand results. Gotta do my best for 'em."

Maeve sighed, and I felt small tugs at the end corners of my duvet. Uh oh. I tightened my grip on the top of the duvet, ready to defend my cozy nest.

"Don't you dare take this duvet! I'm naked under here!"

"If you think I'm afraid of your freckled little butt, you're sadly mistaken," Maeve deadpanned, and yanked the duvet off me in one sharp movement. My tired arms didn't stand a chance at holding it in place.

I lay on my bed, sprawled out in a starfish pose, completely naked with my hair flopped in my face from the force of losing my cocoon. "Why do you hate me?"

"You know that's not what this is. Now get up, I can help out at the site this morning, but I have to call my jackass-lecturer later. So—and I can't believe I'm actually saying this out loud—let's get moving. You'll feel better with some dirt under your nails."

I dragged myself out of bed and shuffled through my morning routine, silently hoping that some fresh air and soil would do me some good. My sour mood hadn't shifted since I got home Saturday night. It was just my luck that Nate and Marcus knew each other and were... friends? Familiar and master? Was that how those things worked? I hadn't heard of a shifter being a familiar to a witch before, but I supposed it wasn't impossible. It definitely wasn't the weirdest thing to happen in this town.

By the time we arrived at the Village Green site, my mood had slightly improved enough that I was ready to get down to some work. I almost wished I hadn't had that kiss with Nate here, just so that I wouldn't be reminded of that wonderful moment every time I looked at Delwyth.

I tried to focus my mind on something else as I worked on laying out markers in the soil, showing where the stone pathway would travel through the site and curl around

Delwyth, linking all the sections of the area. My mind wandered to the last full day I spent here; recalling the phone call I'd had with my mother and the encounter with Marcus.

Ugh, Marcus. That stupid Danger-Noodle. With his intense snake-eyes and infuriating grin. How did he get away with being so damn smug?! It was those cheekbones and that overly relaxed posture. He got to say whatever he wanted because he was gorgeous and he knew it.

Wait, no. Bad thoughts. I needed to think about something else.

Erich. Erich was the exact opposite of Snake-Jerk. He was still attractive, but he was humble about it. He didn't use his hotness to annoy people. He gave thoughtful gifts and made me feel wanted. But he was also human; super off-limits.

Ugh, when did I become so man-crazy?! It was like my vagina was running my brain lately. I needed to find a girlfriend to get me to stop thinking about dick. Why was Maeve straight? She'd have been perfect for me. Damn it.

I settled for keeping my mind busy by singing showtunes with Maeve until she had to head back to the house. She must have been worried about me because she normally hated my singing voice. She usually enjoyed telling me, "You're a Sprite, not a Siren. Stay in your lane, babe." It was harsh, but I knew I wasn't a good singer. Still, today she let me sing my heart out, knowing I needed it. I made a mental note to get some wine for her on the way home tonight.

"Hey, can we talk?"

I turned my head to the cautious voice behind me. Nate stood a few feet away, looking a little paler than the last time I saw him. I wondered if he might have some Scandinavian heritage, with his skin and hair being so light. He had a takeout coffee cup in his hand and the same sad look in his eyes from Saturday night.

"I brought a peace offering, if that helps. I couldn't remember your order, so I took your advice and went for the specials. Did you know they served pumpkin spice lattes in July?"

My mouth quirked up in a smile. It was a thoughtful gesture. I had to remind myself to stay mad at him. "I haven't actually tried one of those yet."

He offered me the cup with the Jewels Cafe logo facing me. "No time like the present, right?"

I wiped the dirt off my hands on my shorts and took the cup from him, feeling weirdly nervous. I didn't know if I was ready to seriously think about this situation with him and Marcus again.

"Thanks. So what did you want to talk about? I mean, I know the subject, obviously, unless you want to talk about the weather or something. I know I'm from the UK and all, but I can't stand weather talk. Sorry, I know I'm rambling. Please, go on."

Nate took a moment to breathe and focus on what he was about to say. I took the pause as a chance to sip the pumpkin spice latte and didn't hate it. It wasn't as sweet as I usually liked my coffee, but it had a wonderful hint of cinnamon, which I loved. It always made me think of fall, with the leaves changing color to beautiful smokey-oranges and reds.

Nate's gaze met mine when he finally spoke. "I need you to know that I had no idea you'd already met Marcus. When I told him I was going out with you before our date, he didn't say anything, so I just assumed you hadn't met."

"Oh, we met all right," I interrupted.

"Yeah, he's... he's a good guy when he wants to be."

"That's not a five-star recommendation there. Tell me, what did he mean the other night when he said he was your familiar? I thought shifters couldn't be familiars; only regular animals could be chosen for that."

"Remember when I told you that blood magic is a little different from regular magic?"

"Yeah, but... Oh. Oh, wow! Did you seriously bind him as a familiar?!" I couldn't believe the words even as I was saying them. I knew that familiars were fairly common among especially powerful witches, but binding a shifter as one was insane to even think about, let alone actually achieve.

Nate crossed and uncrossed his arms, like he couldn't decide what to do with his hands. He settled for putting them in his pockets. "It's not as bad as it sounds, I swear. It was his idea, apparently."

"Apparently? Do you not remember?"

He paused again before looking at me with pleading eyes. "Please don't judge me for this next sentence."

"After everything you've said to me so far, I am absolutely not making that promise."

"That's fair. We were drunk."

"Excuse me?"

"We got drunk with a bunch of friends in university, and I've been told that Marcus dared me to try the spell. He was always pushing me to try to do spells I didn't think I could do. He always did shit like that back then. Still does. Marcus dared me to cast the spell, and by some twist of fate, it actually worked. He's been bound as my familiar ever since."

I took a moment to process the explanation and sipped my coffee again. This was by far the weirdest drunken-night story I'd ever heard. It was like a one-night stand. Only instead of waking up with a few regrets and maybe an STD, they'd woken up with their souls permanently bound together. Unplanned pregnancies had nothing on a supernatural night-out.

"So you guys are just stuck together?"

"Kinda, yeah. He feels pain if he's away from me for too long, but we've lived and worked together for years, so it's not really an issue for us anymore."

"You guys must be really close."

Nate smiled at that, and I could see the relief flash across his face. "Yeah. He's my closest friend. I know he can be a dick sometimes, but he's a great guy, really. I'll level with you, because I'm really trying not to overwhelm you, but I also don't want you getting scared off by another bombshell. We're really close, like we've slept together a lot over the years, even before the spell bound us."

"That's actually not the biggest bombshell you've dropped on me. I'm bisexual. I can deal with you liking guys. I'm just nervous about the guy himself." My fingers picked at the sticker on the side of the coffee cup as I spoke. I wanted to see where things would go with Nate, and I was starting to wonder if I had judged Marcus too harshly in my quick encounters with him.

"Look, I understand if this is too much to deal with. There's literally another person in my life, permanently, but I really like you, Aggy. You have this free-spirit energy about you that makes me feel so at ease around you, and your chest is glowing orange. Why are you glowing orange?"

"Why are you looking at my—oh!" I looked down at my chest, then quickly back up to Nate. "Why am I glowing orange?! I don't glow. That's not a thing for me!"

The glow surrounding my chest started to expand and brighten with each of my breaths, then slowly grew out of me into three distinct strands. Two of the strands faded off in different directions, but the final strand connected straight to Nate's chest. I blinked up in shock as Nate moved his hand back and forth through the glow.

"What the hell is happening right now?" I asked, panic making my voice waver.

"I don't know. Is it connecting us?" Nate turned around and tried to see if the glow was just moving through him. But no matter where he moved, the orange glow stayed firmly fixed from me to him.

"This is too weird. Please tell me this is weird. If this is normal for you, I'm definitely not going on a second date with you."

Nate stopped to look at me again, his face lighting up with surprise. "You're actually up for a second date?"

"Sure, yeah, but can we focus on the weird glowing before planning our next steps as a potential couple?" As I spoke, the strange glow steadily faded like smoke until I had to squint to see it. "Can you still see it? I have to really focus to see."

"Yeah, me too. This is crazy, but I don't think it's harmful." He ran a hand through his overgrown hair with a sigh. "I'm gonna go back to Moonlit Magicks and talk to Bailey. He might know something about spells with orange glows."

"I'll come with you."

"You sure? Marcus was at the shop when I left to come see you."

I took Nate's hand in my own and started leading him away from my work site, throwing my empty coffee cup in the trash can across the street. "I'll deal with him. But I hope you know this doesn't count as the second date, we clear?"

I felt him squeeze my hand as we quickly headed to the shop through town. "Perfectly. How about a trip up the Falls for the second date? I've heard some good things."

I snorted. "Oh, please. You heard it's a make-out spot, didn't you?"

"I'm not answering that without a lawyer present."

We rounded the corner and headed up Main Street, making a beeline straight for Moonlit Magicks. I barely noticed Wallace, the fox shifter, waving a greeting at me as the door to the shop opened and Marcus stepped out. He opened his mouth, probably to say something arrogant, but stopped as the orange glow reappeared and connected his chest to mine, just as Nate's had.

We all took a moment to stare at the glow and, if they were anything like me, freak out in their own heads. So that was where one of the two strands had led to, but where did the last one go?

"Agate? Are those wings on your back?"

I spun on my toes and came face to face with Erich, who had been leaving the store next door. His hands were shaking and his eyes were wide, like he'd just seen a ghost. Or seen wings attached to a girl he'd known for years as wingless.

Wait. He saw my wings?!

And was that the third orange glow connected to his chest?!

CHAPTER EIGHT

I HADN'T SEEN ERICH FOR DAYS UNTIL NOW. IT WAS normal for us. We weren't the kind of friends who had to see or speak to each other every day or else we'd forget about each other. We had an easy rhythm we fell into whenever we met. We had never had any issues between us. The only complication that existed was my hiding my Fae-side from him.

But it looked like that was over now.

Erich looked at me with shock painted across his handsome face. His eyebrows were drawn together as he stared at me with bulging eyes. His mouth hung open, as if the words he'd thought to say had abandoned him. He seemed frozen to the spot. All movement completely halted as he took in the sight of me as I truly was.

A Sprite.

A freak.

Not human.

I didn't know if Erich could see the glowing orange thread of light connecting our chests, but that seemed to be the least of my worries at that moment. My wings twitched slightly, as if they could feel the heavy weight of Erich's stare. I held my hands up in a placating gesture and took a step towards him.

"Erich, I can explain everything."

Erich backed up a step, and I reached out to him, feeling something in my heart pulling towards him. "Please! Please, just talk to me inside for a moment. You know me, I haven't changed."

"You... you have *wings*." His voice was so low it was barely above a whisper.

I heard Marcus's voice from the door to Moonlit Magicks. "Did this guy seriously not know that or something? Also, why are we all glowing? This is new, even for me."

I held back from turning to give Marcus the glare he deserved as Nate spoke up. "He's a human. Shit, we just exposed a damn human and he's not forgetting. Aggy, quick! Bring him inside!"

"Wait, what?" Erich took another step back before I grabbed his hand and used all my strength to drag him inside the store. We needed to avoid any other human eyes seeing what was about to happen. I really didn't want to accidentally traumatize that nice human girl opening the candle store down the road.

"Sorry about this, Erich! I promise I'll explain inside!"

We piled into the shop, and I quickly pulled Erich towards the small room beside the counter. Moonlit Magicks was a surprisingly spacious shop once you were inside. A long glass countertop ran roughly a third of the length of the store, opposite aisles upon aisles of magic supplies. They stocked everything a magic user could require here, from your basic crystals to extremely rare dried animal parts.

Incense filled the air, giving the shop an enchanting atmosphere. Towards the back of the store was a section dedicated to books and felt more like a cozy, old library than a shop. Beyond the book section was a workroom used for brewing potions and casting any spells or enchantments that required a bit more space than the main shop floor offered.

"Hey! That room is for customer consultations only!" Bailey, one of the store owners, yelled out from behind the counter.

"Oh, go consult my little freckled butt, Bailey!" I shouted back and shut the door behind myself and Erich, flicking the lock behind me. I knew that Bailey could easily spell the door open, but I hoped that Nate would talk him down and get me a private moment to talk with Erich.

"Whoa, what the heck is going on, Aggy? Why are you wearing wings and why was that guy talking about me glowing?!"

"Because you *are* glowing." I tried to keep my voice calm and level as I spoke. "I don't know why yet, but I'll tell you everything I do know."

Erich ran a hand down his face and looked at me over his fingers. "Those wings are real, aren't they?"

I gestured to the small couch behind him. "You might want to sit down for this."

The shop's consultation room was tiny; it was just big enough to have a couple of high-back chairs opposite the crimson velvet couch with an antique coffee table between them, and a few wall lamps with mismatching shades. Nothing matched in the room, even the wallpaper looked like it had been left here by the previous building owner in the seventies. The furniture was all antiques bought from Citrine's thrift store, Mystic Thrift, down the street. It was a miracle they'd managed to keep a somewhat fancy Victorian-esque theme here. The room had one small window covered by a thick velvet curtain.

Bailey told me once that the mixture of old furniture and darkness gives the room a "magical ambience". I called bullshit to that. I was convinced he just wanted the room dark so he could nap in here when things were quiet out front.

Erich took a seat on the couch, and I was grateful when he didn't shuffle away from me as I sat next to him, angling my body to face him.

"There's no easy way to tell you this, but I'm a Sprite."

"A Sprite? Like a fairy?" I held back my usual 'not-a-fairy' rant, since Erich was actually quite calm at that moment. There was no need to overwhelm the poor guy more than I was already about to.

"Kind of. Specifically, I'm a Sprite with magic connected to the Earth."

"Earth magic. That sounds pretty perfect for a gardener." I grinned at him, echoing the words I'd said myself to Nate only a few days ago. "You are really a gardener, right? Otherwise, I am definitely going completely insane."

"I'm a gardener, I promise. I'm just a little different from other gardeners. My magic speeds things along a lot, so I can take on pretty big projects without as much help as a human would. I can also talk to plants, and I have an obviously different appearance." I pulled my hair back from where it covered my pointed ears and gestured to my wings. "But I'm actually pretty basic in terms of supernaturals. I can only cast magic relating to the Earth. I don't change shape, I don't have an extended lifespan, and I don't need to eat anything special to live."

Erich took a deep breath in and slowly exhaled. "So what you're saying is that witches, vampires, werewolves... do they seriously exist?"

"They exist. Them and more," I confirm. "You've never seen them around you before because there are wards in this town that make humans ignore magic, or at least forget they saw it. Humans aren't supposed to know about supernaturals."

"But I can see you as you really are now. Y'know, the pointy-ears and wings."

"Yep, that's right. I don't know why, but something similar happened the other night with a kid. The kid didn't glow though, so maybe it's unrelated. I'm so confused by all of this."

"You and me both," he agreed with a long drawn-out sigh, and I instantly felt awful again. He'd been taking it all so well, but I still needed to be more sympathetic. "This is crazy. I mean, I knew you were different, but I didn't think you weren't human! I just thought you were a quirky hippie! I never would have thought any of this."

I decided to give him a moment of quiet to process the information. There wasn't much I felt I could say at that point. All I could do was answer his questions the best I could. I mentally thanked whichever gods were listening that he hadn't stormed out of the room yet.

"Right. So magic is real, you're a Sprite, and the town is filled with supernaturals that I never knew even existed. Is that about it?" Erich looked at me with desperation in his wide, dark eyes, as if he were silently pleading with me not to shake his reality any further.

"You're also glowing orange a bit."

"Oh, how could I forget!? I *glow* now. Why can't I see the glowing, by the way? I can see *you*." He sneered the final word, and I couldn't help but flinch a little. This was more like the reaction I had expected, but that didn't make it hurt less.

"I-I don't know what's causing the glowing. I was at the site with Nate when it started with us and—"

"Yeah, who is that dude, anyway?" Erich interrupted me, and I realized then that I hadn't actually introduced anyone. Oops.

"Nate is a witch. He's a good guy. We were talking next to Delwyth, and he saw that my chest was glowing."

"Why was he looking at your chest? Wait, no. Focus on the glowing and why I can't see it, for now."

I wondered if I should be flattered or concerned by everyone's attention to my chest. It wasn't like there was much to look at there. I was so flat, I didn't even need to wear a bra most days.

"The glowing spread out from me into three strands. One of them connected from me to Nate, another to his friend in the other room—the slouching loudmouth—and the last one connected me to you. I didn't even realize it until we met in the street just now."

"Is that weird for you? I'm trying to gauge how worried I should be."

"It's weird for me. Nate and I were hoping to get some answers here, but we bumped into you and... well, this happened. I'm sorry for not telling you about me, I really am." My voice cracked as I apologized.

I needed him to know that I never meant for any of this to happen. I had desperately tried to keep his safe, human life away from the craziness of magic for years. Only for it all to be spoiled for a reason I didn't even understand myself.

The unfairness of the situation made me want to cry, but I knew it wouldn't help anything. I had to focus on helping Erich understand the magical world or he wouldn't stand a chance out there.

"Does Maeve know?"

"Yeah, she knows. She's like me, actually. She's a Gnome."

"A *Gnome*?!" If Erich had been drinking something at that moment, it would have been a perfect spit-take. I loved it when people found out about Maeve, the reactions were always hilarious. But I held in my laughter. "Like the little old man statues with the fishing rods and pointy hats?"

I bit my lip, trying desperately to keep a straight face. "Yep. Though if you make that comparison in front of her, I guarantee she'll sock you in the mouth with zero hesitation."

There was a long moment of silence as I watched Erich's expression filter from shock to uncontrollable laughter. I let myself join in, finally able to let the giggles out.

"Oh, wow!" Erich relaxed back into the couch and tilted his head back, looking up at the ceiling. "Damn, none of this makes any sense. But it feels really good to laugh with you again, Aggy."

He reached across my lap and picked up my pale hand in his darker one, entwining our fingers together. I rested my spare hand on top of our hands and leaned forward, resting my forehead on his shoulder and inhaling his scent deeply. He always smelled like lavender from the plants his grandfather kept in the house they shared. Erich used the plants to make air fresheners for his delivery van. He always said the scent was homey and relaxed him. I completely understood why as I breathed in the scent. I had been so close to losing him, but I always felt so safe around him.

"Are you mad at me?" I spoke in a small voice, a little scared of the answer.

"No." He sounded confident in that firm statement. "I'm not mad, but this is going to take some time for me to get used to."

"Thank you, Erich. I mean it. I really don't know what I'd do if I lost you." I squeezed his hand a little as I spoke, relieved when he squeezed mine back.

Erich shifted in his seat at my words, turning to look at me as I sat up straighter. He took a moment to really look at me for the first time since he found out about me, and his expression softened. His eyes flicked from my wings, to my pointed ears, to my eyes, and I met his gaze with a confidence I wouldn't have been able to muster while still pretending to be human.

Our lips connected softly, barely grazing each other before pressing together firmly and finally getting a taste for each other after years of wondering.

A sharp knock sounded at the door as Nate's deep voice filtered through the wood. "Hey, you guys okay?"

We separated from the kiss as I raised my voice so Nate could hear me outside. "Yeah, we'll be out now in a minute!"

"You'll be out when?"

Erich chuckled as we stood up and moved to unlock and open the door. "It's a Welsh thing she says. I don't get it either, but you'll get used to it."

I stood between them with my mouth open in mock-offense. "*Excuse* me, it makes perfect sense!"

"Yeah, to you." Erich smiled at me, and I was relieved to see the smile actually reach his eyes this time.

Nate turned to Erich and asked cautiously. "So you're okay? Aggy told you everything?"

Erich nodded. "Yeah. It's pretty bizarre, and I'm not totally sure that I'm not insane, but why don't we go find out why we're all glowing."

CHAPTER NINE

I LEFT THE CONSULTATION ROOM TO FIND BAILEY glaring at me from behind the glass counter and Marcus leaning against the wall beside him, an infuriating smirk plastered across his face. He looked like the annoying sibling who hid behind their favorite parent to taunt you when you were getting scolded by them.

"I don't appreciate you commandeering my consultation room, Aggy. Next time your 'little freckled butt' wants to expose the magical community, kindly do it in your treehouse." Bailey's glare beamed dangerously at me as he used the air quotes.

He usually looked fairly harmless, with his lanky stature and pastel pink hair covering his pointed Fae ears, but there was a burning fire in Bailey that I knew to watch out for. As a half-Fae, half-witch hybrid, Bailey was as magically powerful as he was verbally fierce.

"Lay off her, Bay, it was an emergency and you know it," Nate reasoned from behind me.

"Doesn't mean I have to be happy about it." Bailey's glare softened into a slight pout. As quick as he was to antagonize people around him, he wasn't great at taking it himself.

"Aww, no, be mad again! I was having fun watching Agatha squirm." Marcus's snake eyes flashed with mischief as he moved away from the wall and came around to our side of the counter.

Erich leaned down to whisper in my ear. "Please tell me he's not the other glowing guy you were talking about."

"Yes, little human, I am the other member of this misfit group. Shifters have excellent hearing, by the way." He gave Erich a wink before rounding his gaze back onto me. "Now, Agatha, what mess have you dragged me into?"

"Me? You think this is *my* fault?! And stop calling me that! You know my name."

Marcus swaggered towards me, leaning over me and pointing at my chest where, if I focused, I could still see the glowing remnants of that unknown spell. "*You*, my dear, are at the center of whatever this is. It's not connecting us to each other, it's connecting us to you. Looks like you can't keep avoiding me anymore."

He grinned down at me, far too close for my liking, but I didn't want to give him the satisfaction of making me step away. He infuriated me, making my heart pound with rage every time I was near him. He circled around to lean against the shelf behind me, and I swear I could feel his eyes tracking all over me.

"Dude, please stop that creepy attempt at flirting, it's making me nauseous." Bailey rolled his eyes and pulled his phone out of his pocket. "Have any of you checked Screech this morning?"

"Screech?" Erich asked.

"It's an app for supernaturals. It's a combo of news, socials, reviews, and other stuff. They just started doing food delivery too," I answered, happy for the distraction. I turned back to Bailey. "What's going on?"

"Your handsome man here isn't the only human noticing magic today. There's a few reports of shifters and spells being seen, mostly by kids. They've been freaking out and running away, then going back to normal pretty soon after."

"Sounds just like that kid who saw you the other night," Nate noted.

"The other night? But you said earlier that the glowing only started about an hour ago."

"Yeah, that's right," I confirmed. "Which means the two probably aren't related and we actually have two magical problems. Wonderful."

"Bailey, what do you know about glowing orange threads? This is the first time I've seen them," Nate asked, staying a lot calmer than I was. This situation was getting crazier every minute, and all I wanted to do was go sit under a tree and breathe for a while.

"They're pretty common around here, actually. I've seen a few people with remnants of those kinds of spells, but I don't actually know what they are or where they come from. Look it up or something. Use the brain I hired you for."

Bailey had a point, as rude as he was about it. We were in a magic shop with a built-in library of spell books. It made sense to do a little research while we were here, but we still didn't have any leads on why humans were seeing supernaturals.

Nate started walking towards the books and crooked his finger at Marcus. "Come on, you're with me. Let's look for glowy things."

"Yes, sir." Marcus gave Nate a sloppy salute, turned to

give me one last wink, then followed Nate down to the bookshelves. Cocky jerk.

While Bailey went back to working on his laptop behind the counter, I pulled my phone out of the back pocket of my shorts and scrolled through the posts on Screech. There weren't many—which was a relief—but it was strange.

The wards around the town prevented humans, and those unaware of magic, from being able to see anything paranormal. There were similar wards in towns all over the world. They were usually small communities or sometimes they were universities, which were specific to supernaturals. Places like this allowed supes to learn to master our powers until they were capable enough to blend into human society on their own without risk of exposure.

"Hey, Bailey, is it possible for the town's wards to fail?"

The spells that created the wards were old, I knew that much. People always took them for granted. We never had to boost them or make new ones, but theoretically, all spells could end, eventually.

Bailey snorted at my question, but didn't look up from his laptop as he responded. "Fail? No. Those things have been around since before the town was even built. No one knows who made 'em. Our buddy Christian wrote his damn thesis on the function of wards like this town has. I don't remember the details because I'm not a nerd, but his conclusion was something along the lines of 'they're old, don't touch'."

"But what if someone touched?"

Bailey let out a long sigh and flipped the screen down on his laptop, reluctantly giving me his full attention. "Where would you even touch those wards, Aggy? No one has been able to figure out where or how they were cast, they're that old. Even the local vampires are clueless because none of them know anyone who was alive here back then. Unless you have a source we don't, the wards are fine."

"What about on Halloween?" Marcus spoke up from the other side of the store, surprising both Bailey and myself. I needed to keep reminding myself that he had shifter hearing, but doing that would keep him in my mind. Ugh, decisions.

"What's on Halloween?" Erich asked, desperately trying to keep up with the conversation.

"It was one of the selling points for moving here. There's that huge Halloween party. You said it was a human-supe social or something, I dunno." Marcus gestured to Bailey to continue as he went back to looking at books with Nate.

"Yeah, it is. I'd never thought about it before, but the wards come down around the venue for the annual Halloween Ball."

"I never normally go to that. Maeve and I usually stay home and watch horror movies. But the wards actually come *down*? Like they stop working completely?!"

Bailey shrugged his shoulders. "I don't know how it works. I think it's a council thing. All I know is humans see supernaturals inside the venue and just think it's a costume. It lets us relax a bit, y'know. Then they're back to normal later. No specific memories of the event, just a feeling that they had fun."

Erich nodded. "I've been a few times, but I don't remember seeing anything crazy. I've just always had a fun night."

"Exactly. There's no fuss, and if the humans leave the area, they forget it all early, anyway. It's a once-a-year spell, and it barely lasts six hours. It's not what we're looking for."

I bit my bottom lip and tried to think about things carefully. I'd felt so sure I was on to something there. Erich's hand gently landed on my shoulder and snapped me out of my thoughts. "It's okay, Aggy. We'll figure this out. Well, you guys will, but I'll help where I can. I'm not going anywhere."

"I mean I really wish you would go somewhere else," Bailey muttered.

Deciding to completely ignore Bailey's snide comment, I hugged Erich tightly. His arms circled my shoulders, giving me a gentle squeeze, and I noticed that he didn't touch my back like he usually did. He was avoiding my wings. The realization stung my heart as I swallowed around a lump in my throat. His lavender scent didn't give me any of the comfort it usually did.

"Thanks, Erich. Why don't you take a look around here while I go check on Nate. We'll figure out some next steps."

As I padded my way down the store to the book section, I didn't worry about leaving my dirty footprints. Bailey had ticked me off today and deserved the cleanup.

I wondered where Ellis was today. He was usually in the shop with Bailey, but maybe today was his day off. He could probably afford to take one day off more often now that Nate and Marcus were here to help out. Come to think of it, what did Marcus do in the shop? He wasn't a witch, and as far as I was aware, he didn't have any magic except for his connection to Nate. Maybe he stocked shelves. Or maybe he spent his time lounging in the sun, ready to annoy unsuspecting Sprites. Either was pretty likely.

I decided to quietly hover over the floor so Marcus wouldn't hear me sneaking up on them. It was time for a little payback. Nate and Marcus had moved to the far corner of the shop, so I silently crept closer, glad that my wings didn't make any flapping or buzzing noises. The only thing they caused was a gentle breeze.

I stopped at the end of a bookcase when I could hear the two of them speaking in low voices. They hadn't noticed me, so I silently lowered myself to the ground and listened to their voices.

Was I being unnecessarily sneaky? Yes.

Was I going to do it, anyway? Also, yes.

I heard Nate grumbling first. "Seriously, dude, you have to stop pissing her off."

"I'll stop messing with her when it stops being funny."

"Come on, you said it yourself, we're connected to her, and right now we don't know how or why. We need her, and you're just pushing her away. This is serious magic, Marcus, the kind with unknown consequences."

Marcus scoffed and responded in the most sarcastic voice he could summon. "Oh no. What shall I do? I have absolutely no experience of being bound to another person as the consequence of serious magic, none whatsoever."

"This is exactly why she thinks you're a jerk."

"Actually, I know for a fact that she thinks I'm sexy. Her pheromones skyrocket whenever I'm near her. Speaking of..." He raised his voice a little, so he spoke clearly to me. "Are you going to hide behind that shelf all day or just until we stop talking about you, Tinkerbell?"

He knew I'd been hiding there the whole time?! Damn shifter senses. I thought I'd stayed far enough away that he wouldn't be able to sense me.

I walked over to them, staying close to Nate and avoiding eye contact with Marcus, who was grinning ear to ear. "Thanks for trying to get him to back off, Nate."

"Anytime, Aggy." He reached up and tucked the hair that had fallen out from my headband back behind my ear. His hand lingered in my hair as he asked me, "How's Erich handling things?"

"He's okay, but he's gonna need time to process everything. We hugged just now and he couldn't touch my wings now he knows they're there. Not gonna lie, that hurt, but it's not exactly unexpected." I shrugged my shoulders sadly and leaned into Nate. He wrapped his arms around me, holding me close without worrying about touching my wings like Erich had.

This is what I'd needed. There was something so comforting about Nate's embrace as I listened to the thumping of his heartbeat against my ear. We still knew so little about each other, but being held by him felt so right.

As I was thinking this, a second set of arms wrapped around me and I felt a chin rest on top of my head. The body behind me pressed up tightly, pushing Nate a little off balance and making him lean against the bookcase on the wall.

"Really, dude?" Nate asked.

"What? I thought this was a group hug for our darling Sprite. Besides, she fits so well between us, don't you think?"

My cheeks quickly heated at that comment so I squished my face against Nate's shirt to hide them, surrounding myself in his tempting scent. The worst thing was that the heat radiating from Marcus's body at my back wasn't unpleasant. Not at all. Though it didn't help that the only clothing covering my behind were my shorts and the piece of shirt covering my lower back. I was sure I could feel him grinning above my head, but all my brain wanted to focus on was the two rock hard chests boxing me in between them.

Nate's arms were getting slightly crushed against my back with Marcus pressing in. They felt so close, I was pretty sure they could feel each other's breath above my head. Nate had said before that they'd slept together a bunch of times, so I supposed having me pressed between them like this wasn't going to make them uncomfortable. In fact, they'd likely enjoy it more if we were all wearing less clothing.

Wait. No! Bad thoughts!

"I think you like that thought, Sweetheart. Being sandwiched between us like this must give you all sorts of ideas," Marcus whispered in my ear and gave the delicate pointed tip a nip between his teeth.

I swirled around in their combined embrace and looked up at Marcus vehemently. The audacity of this man, I swear! He took the opportunity to firmly cup my jaw between his thumb and index finger and hold my gaze up at him, making sure I couldn't look away. The moment his bare skin touched mine, at least half my anger left my body, replaced with lust. There was something about him that seemed to equally enchant me and piss me off.

"Well, that answers that."

He leaned down to me close enough that our noses brushed each other. Nate's hands moved down to my hips and squeezed a little, letting me know he was there, pressed behind me, but I couldn't tell whose side he was on. Was he telling me to hold my ground and let Marcus know where to shove it? Or did he want Marcus to kiss me? Too much was happening for my brain to process everything, and yet, no one had moved for several heartbeats.

My leaf-green eyes stared up into Marcus's amber snake

eyes. My eyes often changed color on their own to match the shade of the tree leaves in the area. It was odd, but I didn't think that was what he was interested in.

Marcus focused intently on me, as if he were looking for something specific in my gaze, just like that day in the Village Green last week. His nostrils flared as he scented me, and I remembered him doing the same in his python-form with the little tongue-flicker when he had me pinned. What was he trying to figure out?

His eyes widened a little, as if something clicked in his mind. I really didn't like that look. There was something very dangerous about him knowing something I didn't.

"So that's it. Very interesting," he mused.

I swallowed around a lump in my throat and found my voice. "What are you talking about?"

"Calm your heart rate, Sunshine. It's nothing bad. Well, not for me, for sure. It's reassuring actually, considering your reactions to me."

"Tell me!"

"Oh, well, when I'm near you your heart goes wild and frankly you lose all sense. But you already know that."

"Tell me *what it means*," I practically growled in his face, and his expression somehow managed to grow wilder. My hands balled into fists as I struggled not to lash out. This was infuriating, and he knew exactly what he was doing to me.

The corner of his mouth tilted up in a smirk as he licked over his lower lip. "It means, you're attracted to me, silly. It's nice, actually, I'm glad my mate thinks I'm a hot piece of ass."

My mouth dropped open in shock. Oh. Fuck my life.

Sprites didn't have fated mates the way shifters did. We never had that one perfect soulmate who complimented us perfectly. But that didn't mean we couldn't be chosen as the mate of a shifter. It was extremely rare, but it did happen.

Marcus took full advantage of my shock and closed the fraction of space between us, kissing me firmly enough that my head bumped back against Nate's chest. I felt Nate's hands tighten on each of my hips, but he made no move to stop what was happening. If anything, I think he was enjoying the front row seat to this show.

My fists reached up, gripping the front of Marcus's shirt, though I wasn't sure if I planned to push him away or pull him closer. His lips moved against mine with a searing heat, and I found myself kissing him back. It all felt so right, but my mind was screaming at me.

Marcus didn't go any further, having at least that much common sense in the moment. He nipped my bottom lip as he slowly pulled away, and my hands dropped to my sides. Nate's grip on my hips loosened, though he didn't let go completely. It was as if he was afraid I'd launch myself at Marcus, either in lust or rage.

It was a good call, really.

A sharp smack echoed through the shop, and it took me a moment to realize that my hand was stinging from the impact against Marcus's cheek.

"Everything okay back there?" Bailey's voice called out from the front of the store.

Marcus chuckled as he brought his hand up to his cheek, now pink from my solid hit. "Yep! Nothing I didn't deserve!"

"You really did deserve that," Nate noted, and Marcus shrugged a response.

"Don't be so jealous I found a mate. You'll always be my first mystical bond, Nathaniel."

"You're so sweet when you choose to be."

CHAPTER TEN

The ring of the bell above the store's front door interrupted me from causing any more of a scene in the back of the store. Though I had a fair few obscenities locked and loaded if Marcus kept up his "annoy the Sprite" act.

"Honey, I'm home!" Ellis, the second owner of Moonlit Magicks—and Maeve's chaotic ex—announced as he walked in. He was a tall, tanned man with dark tattoos swirling up both of his arms, reaching his neck. Each tattoo was a symbol he used as part of his witchcraft. He specifically practised alchemy, though I didn't know what most of them meant.

"Thank the gods you're back, El. Nate brought in a stray, who brought in a human, and they're all cursed or some shit. It's stressing me the hell out." I could hear Bailey's whine from the back of the store, so I moved back to the front desk, flanked by Nate and my apparent mate, to see if Ellis would know anything.

Erich poked out from one of the aisles along the way and checked on me. "You okay, Aggy? You look flustered."

"I'm fine, or at least I will be. Probably. Things are messier than I thought." I forced a smile to try to reassure him, but even I wasn't convinced by it.

"Aggy! Good to see you! I didn't know you knew Nate." Ellis came over and gave me a quick hug. Despite his bizarre relationship with Maeve, we were friendly towards each other. I actually thought he was a good guy; the two of them were just a terrible influence on each other.

"Hey, El. Yeah, we met last week. Quick question for you; do you know anything about orange glowing threads linking people?"

"Like the one I can see on you guys right now? It's a mate spell."

The room was suddenly deadly silent. Ellis looked at me as if he had no idea the gravity of what he'd just said to me. We were both distracted by Bailey howling with laughter from his position behind the counter.

"Oh, *wow*! You guys are so fucked! I don't even know which of you I feel more sorry for!" Bailey howled with glee.

I inhaled a deep breath and let it out slowly. "Ellis. Explain it to me very slowly and carefully. What exactly does a mate spell do?"

"Uh, it reveals a mate connection, like it makes it visible. Usually just to magic users, though. Did you guys not know about your spell?"

"Nope."

"There, you see? We're all meant to be!" Marcus sounded thrilled, but I was pretty sure he was just enjoying watching my mental breakdown happen right in front of him.

"Wait, a 'mate' connection? Like soulmates?" Erich asked.

Nate kept his voice level, but it sounded like even he was struggling to come to terms with our situation. "Yeah, yeah, like soulmates. Witches don't normally get them, same for humans. It's usually a shifter thing. Oh, wow."

"This can't be happening. There's just no way..." As a Sprite, I shouldn't have one mate, let alone three of them. "You're seriously telling me that fate gave me three soulmates? And they're *all men*?! What the actual hell!"

"You seriously want more people involved in this?" Marcus asked, raising an eyebrow. I couldn't tell if he was enjoying the idea of more people or not.

"I'm just saying a woman would've been nice, is all. Ugh, I hate it when Maeve is right! I really am destined for dick!"

"Technically, you're destined for *dicks*. Plural."

"Oh, I'm well aware of the number of dicks surrounding me right now!"

Everyone around me flinched as I yelled my frustrations and started pacing around the store. My head was a flurry of panicked thoughts.

Poor Erich had only just found out about this entire world an hour ago and now fate had determined that he was not only the soulmate of a girl with wings, but that same girl would have two other guys who are apparently perfect for her.

Perfect. That was a laugh. In what world was Marcus my perfect match? Unless Nate was the match and Marcus got dragged along by the familiar bond? No, that was too much of a stretch, even by magical terms.

I supposed that rejecting the connection was possible. That was a thing, right? But I'd heard that shifters who rejected their mates were almost never happy later in life. It was described like losing a limb. I wondered if I could live with that, but could they? This was completely insane.

Oh my Goddess, I really was stuck with these men.

"Her face looks really weird right now," Nate muttered.

Marcus nodded in agreement. "Is she constipated or something?"

"No, I think I've seen this one before. It's either her heartburn face, or she's thinking of the best place to hide a body. They look really similar," Erich explained.

I paused in my pacing and looked over to the guys doing their commentary on my face. During my lengthy freakout, they'd assembled in front of the counter and watched me like I was some kind of exhibit they were concerned would spontaneously combust from stress. How was I the only one freaking out? I thought at least Erich would have joined my panic, but he now seemed perfectly at ease with fate's cruel idea of a joke.

"How are you all so calm right now?" I asked, my voice squeaking from my shock.

Marcus winked at me. "Like I said before, this isn't my first magical rodeo. Though I think being magically bonded to three different people might be my limit. I like to think I'm a very open-minded person."

Erich looked from Marcus to me and shrugged. "Honestly? I think I've been so worked up that I've now looped back around to calm. I'll probably freak out again later, though. I might go scream in the woods or something. That's what people usually do in this situation, right?"

That was understandable. I was impressed by how well he was dealing with all of this compared to me. I felt like my world was crumbling around me, leaving me with three men who I wasn't sure I wanted to spend my life with, but who fate seemed to think were my perfect match.

Erich had actually just had the predictable rug of

human life pulled out from under him, leaving him to land on the hard floor of magical reality. You would think it would be a fluffy, somehow sparkly landing, but things in the magical world often weren't as soft and squishy as you'd think. All things considered, he was coping remarkably well. Too well. I should have been able to cope that well. Why couldn't I cope well?!

My feet were moving again before I realized what I was doing. I'd managed to create a dirty trail in a figure-eight pattern around two aisles of magical equipment with my feet. Walking helped me think, and I needed to know what to do about this spell on me. Where did it even come from? Did I always have it? Did something trigger it?

Nate stepped forward and put his hands on my shoulders, stopping me in my tracks as I completed another lap. "It's going to be okay, Aggy. On the scale of problems in this town, this one is pretty low."

"Ugh, you're right. I hate that you're right. I hate that I'm freaking out so badly. Again. I hate all of this!"

"Do you hate me?"

I looked up at Nate, shocked at the blunt nature of the question. "What? No!"

He started rubbing his thumbs over my shoulders, the movement surprisingly soothing. "That's a great start. Do you like me?"

My eyes narrowed as I stared up at him. I answered slowly, trying to predict where he was going with this, but not having any luck. "Yes, I like you."

"Good, it would have been super awkward if you'd said 'no' to my face like that." We laughed together a little. It was amazing. Nate had a gift for bringing out the joy in me. "Do you hate Marcus? Or Erich?"

I had to think about the first part of that question. "No, I don't hate either of them."

"We don't have to rush into anything with this mate-thing. Remember what Ellis said; the spell only reveals the potential. It doesn't force us into anything. We can take things as slow as we need to and just see how things feel."

That sounded good. I really didn't want to rush into any life-altering decisions while I was reeling from these revelations, and it would be good for Erich to have time to get used to the magical world being his new normal for a while. I might even get used to Marcus. He seemed to be a package deal with Nate because of the familiar bond.

I knew I wasn't ready to commit to a relationship, let alone a relationship with three people—two of whom I had only met last week. I had only just started dating again, and suddenly I was thrown into this huge mess of life-changing relationships.

"Okay. We'll shelve that for now. What are we going to do about the humans seeing magic?"

"Did you say your hometown had a similar warding spell as we do here?" I nodded, impressed that Nate had remembered that little fact. "Is there someone there you can call who might know how the spell works?"

"You're basically asking me to call my *mam*. Hard pass." I refused to open that can of worms again so soon. If I called my mother, we'd probably just end up arguing again. Worse, I might accidentally let this soulmate situation slip, and then she would be even more unbearable. I wondered if that would be the thing that would actually make her visit me here. Oh, please, no.

"I suppose we could contact the Paranormal Council, but that might just cause a panic. Especially if it's something easily fixed." Nate pondered the thought for a moment. "We should look for areas in town with especially high concentrations of magic. Check the flow?"

"Excuse me?" Erich asked. In all fairness to him, I was confused by the theory behind this idea too.

"Magic has a certain flow in towns like this, like a river. Towns like this are usually built on top of ley lines, which increases the potency of magic and the effectiveness of wards encompassing a large area. Natural landforms on ley lines generally have a very high concentration of this power, almost like the water is behind a dam. It's why a lot of witches do rituals in certain areas," Nate explained, and I found myself following pretty well.

Erich was nodding his head like he understood perfectly, but Marcus looked like he was ignoring the whole conversation in favor of scrolling on his phone.

"I mean the town is called Moonlit Falls. Would the waterfalls be one of these power-place things?" Erich asked.

I was suddenly so proud of him. He really did catch onto things quickly. Maybe he would adapt to the magical world better than I initially thought.

Nate grinned, clearly as proud of Erich as I was. "Most likely, yes. Didn't you say there are two main waterfalls in town, Bailey?"

Bailey nodded, muttering something under his breath. I knew he was getting desperate for us all to get out of the shop now. Every time he rolled his eyes, a puppy took a shit on a rug somewhere.

"Yes, they link together along the river. You have the big Cupid Falls up the trail past the northern woods, on the edge of town, and Moonlit Falls down along the river rapids. You can see Moonlit Falls outside through the back window. But just saying, I've never felt anything magical outside from the normal waterfall-energy from those, so Cupid Falls is probably your best bet."

Nate turned to smile at me. "Looks like I'm taking you on that second date sooner than we thought."

"Huh? We're all going on a date?" Marcus piped up, clearly only listening for keywords.

I ignored him, looking out the front window instead. The sky was still blue, but it wasn't going to stay that way for long. "It's getting late. By the time we get to Cupid Falls, we would only have a couple of hours of sunlight. It would be better to go first thing in the morning."

"Does that mean you can all leave my shop now?"

"Stop whining, Bay." Ellis chuckled. He was always amused by Bailey's frantic switch from sassy to grumposaurus-rex. "But we should probably get the word out to the other supernaturals about the humans seeing things in town. Y'know, before someone notices the Bigfoot who runs the thrift store down the street."

"Hey, she's a nice lady!" I shouted a little too loudly, then quickly composed myself. "I'll get the word out to my gardening clients and tell them to be careful with their magic. I'll ask them to spread it to their contacts and so on. Hopefully, some of the more physically-obvious supes stay home for a few days. I should probably lie low too."

"Good idea, Aggy. I mean, don't get me wrong, you're adorable, but you do stand out pretty easily." Nate smiled to try and soften the blow.

"Yeah, you're right. I'll go straight home. I should be fine once I get to the woods. Hardly anyone lives near me."

Nate pulled me into a quick hug, gently kissing the top of my head. "Just be careful, okay?"

"I will be, don't worry."

"Good. We'll all meet on the bridge tomorrow and make the hike up to Cupid Falls."

Mumbled agreements filled the room until a loud sigh followed from Bailey. "Will you all please leave already?! Your antics have been scaring away my customers all afternoon!"

CHAPTER ELEVEN

The next day, I made my way carefully through the forest to the edge of town, then stuck closely to side streets to avoid being seen. Even while avoiding human eyes, I noticed the town was a lot quieter than usual. I didn't hear nearly as much chatter in the streets. Random laughs, or even the occasional scream were both pretty normal, but things were eerily quiet. Hopefully, it meant that word had successfully got out to the majority of supernaturals and they were playing it safe for a day or so.

I spotted Erich standing in the middle of the bridge, looking over the edge at Starlight River and the tumbling rapids of Moonlit Falls as they made their way towards the center of town, and waved him over to me. It was better for me to stay with my back to the buildings for now.

"Hey, Aggy, you okay?"

"Yep, I'm so glad we agreed to meet close to noon today. I think yesterday exhausted me way more than I realized. I slept like the dead. But more importantly, how are you? Are you coping with things okay? I'm a little surprised you managed to get the day off work."

Erich nodded and fiddled with the strap of his backpack. His expression was unsure. He was biting a little on the inside of his cheek, which didn't exactly fill me with confidence, but he forced a smile. "Yeah, work was fine with me taking some vacation time. Getting home yesterday was an experience, though. I wouldn't have thought that Spinel had a horn, that was a bit of a shock."

I chuckled to myself. "Yep, she's a unicorn. Like a legit unicorn. Even I was surprised when I saw her. I was always taught in school that they were only native to Scotland, but here she is. I guess my teacher didn't get out of the valley much."

"You were taught that in school? So, wait, are there supernatural schools?"

"That's right. Mine was a little different, though. I went to a Fae-only school from Primary years all the way up to what you'd call High School. Maeve's school had a whole bunch of different supes, which is why our schools were paired together for a pen-pal project."

"I remember you mentioned that before, but knowing the magic behind it makes even more sense now." He took a deep breath and looked back towards the river from where we were standing. "It's strange. Things are crazier than ever for me now, but the things around me are also making a crazy amount of sense. Is that weird?"

I shook my head and adjusted the tote bag on my shoulder. "No, your eyes are just open now. It's like high-definition television, only the details you were missing were magic."

"That's a good way to put it. It's just going to take some getting used to. I'm trying not to stare at people that I've known for my whole life like they're entirely new people. I know they're the same inside, like you are."

That was such a relief to hear. I had been so afraid of Erich judging me for my wings, or being so disgusted that he'd never speak to me again. It looked like sleeping on it had really helped him process it all. It was a good sign for whatever future this town held for him.

"Hey, you two!" Nate called from down the street. He was walking up the road towards us, one hand holding onto the strap of a backpack, with Marcus swaggering up alongside him empty handed. "Sorry we couldn't leave earlier, we had a few things to do in the shop before Bailey would let us escape. He said something about the fate of the town kissing his ass, I wasn't listening."

"No problem. Are you ready for the hike?" Erich asked them both, slightly eyeing up Marcus, who was dressed in tight jeans. Not the best hiking outfit, but then again, I was barefoot in a loose dress with a tote bag. I had no right to judge.

Nate grinned his excitement, motioning to his backpack. "Yep, I brought snacks for all of us, just in case."

"Nice! Me too!" Erich exclaimed as I watched the two of them share a strange moment of bonding over their boy scout-like behavior. It was actually kind of cute.

Stepping in front of them, I waved them towards the bridge. "If you guys are ready, I'll take you up a path I know on the west side of the bridge up to Cupid Falls. There are usually less people on that path since it's a bit farther from the town, but it'll get us to the same place. Come on."

We crossed the bridge quickly, with me tucked between Erich and Nate to hide my wings as best as we could, then headed into the forest where we were able to space out a bit again. We walked in relative silence, absorbing the sounds around us. I didn't mention it to the guys, but the real reason I wanted to take this route up to the Falls was because I just preferred it. I saw the Eastern forest every day going to and from home. This was more of a luxury for me.

The sun was shining brightly on the path in front of us, the trees not as dense here. Branches creaked in the wind as we moved through the underbrush, and I found myself smiling at the sensation of fresh moss between my toes. I took a moment to look around above me, seeing a small family of birds silhouetted against the sky as they flew between the trees, and noticed Nate watching me out of the corner of my eye.

"Everything okay?"

He nodded, almost shaking himself out of his trance. "Yeah, it's just incredible watching you in your element. Sorry for the pun."

I snorted. "That was a pretty painful pun, but you're forgiven."

"Thanks. But like I said, seeing you like this—surrounded by woodland and greenery—it suits you. You said once that you live in the woods, right? Is your house near here?"

"No, I live on the other side of the river. My house is about halfway between the town and Cupid Falls."

"Wait, so you doubled back just to take us up to the Falls?" Nate asked.

I grinned and moved with more of a bounce in my step. "Well, yeah. You would totally get lost without me. Even locals like Erich don't know the forests as well as I do. Well, obviously Garnet knows them, but I'm a very close second. Besides, you'd miss out on all these beautiful trees if you'd taken the basic route. Aren't they incredible?"

I closed my eyes as I walked, feeling the path with my toes, and listened to the whispers of the trees surrounding me. I couldn't hear their exact words without being closer to them and focusing unless they decided to yell at me, but there was something comforting about being able to hear their mumbling. It was a reminder of just how alive the forest was.

"Hey! Be careful, Tinkerbell!"

I froze in place at Marcus's panicked voice and turned to face him. "What's wrong?"

He pointed in front of us to where there was a large puddle of thick, boggy mud stretching across the path and down farther into the trees. "You were about to step right into that stuff! You really couldn't wear shoes for this? Come on, we'll find a way around it."

I couldn't hold back my laughter. "You're kidding, right? The ground feels so good! Seriously, you should try it." I walked on, straight through the mud that went up to my mid-calves, and cackled to myself as I heard all three guys groan at how gross it was. I looked back at them with a grin plastered across my face.

"C'mon, it's fun! People pay good money for mud like this. Plus, it makes such a satisfying squelchy-sound!"

"You're disgusting. Like, you might actually be the first shifter-mate to permanently kill a boner." Marcus cringed as he watched each of my steps through the mud.

I flipped him off with both hands, not breaking my grin, and jumped a little in the mud, enjoying the squishy texture as much as I was enjoying the horrified looks on each of their faces.

Marcus looked at Nate and Erich with a sour expression. "Are we really mated to that?"

"Yep. We're pretty much stuck with her now, buddy." Nate patted him on the shoulder and went to step in the mud and catch up with me.

"Wait!" Nate turned back around as Marcus shifted into his python form and wrapped himself around Nate's shoulders. The lengths this man was going through to avoid some mud was equal parts impressive and concerning.

Nate and Erich steadily started trudging through the mud, trying to keep mostly at the edges where it wasn't as deep. But I was pretty sure I heard Erich mutter about how some had made it into his sock. Marcus stayed curled up around Nate's shoulders, twisting around one of his biceps. I was shocked by the size of his python form, now that I could see him as more than a set of teeth in front of my face. He must have been at least fifteen feet long. It was hard to tell, and frankly, I was too nervous to ask.

I noticed Marcus's stunning amber eyes looking around the forest leisurely and, occasionally, following me. I remembered how he'd yelled for me to stop before I went in the mud and how he'd sounded genuinely concerned for a brief moment. Maybe there was more to this mate bond than I'd originally thought.

As the ground dried out and we started walking on regular dirt and moss again, Marcus shifted back, landing softly on the ground. Erich stared at him as he stood there, back in his human form, but with his snake eyes remaining. Those seemed to be permanent, from what I'd seen.

"Why aren't you naked?"

"Excuse me?" Marcus's eyebrows rose sharply at Erich's question. In all fairness, I hadn't seen that one coming either.

"When you changed back—which was very cool, by the way—why do you still have clothes? I mean, where do your clothes go when you're a snake?" It was a valid question. Most shifters ended up naked after shifting, unless they were magically powerful enough for it to not be an issue, or if they used specific spells or talismans.

"It's because of the bond to Nate. I'm his familiar, so I carry a portion of his magic for emergencies. It also gives me the ability to shift without losing the clothes I was wearing in my human form." Marcus shrugged, like it was no big deal. "I don't know exactly how it works, but I couldn't do it before we bonded."

"Huh. So that's what a familiar does." Considering the shock of seeing my wings for the first time, Erich handled a shape-shifting python-man with tremendous ease. I guess since he already knew it was a possibility, he'd had the chance to mentally prepare. Still, I was impressed with him.

"Come on!" I called out to them. "We're not far away now. If you listen, you can hear the Falls from here."

We moved quickly towards the sound of rushing water until we reached the spacious open glade at the base of Cupid Falls. It was a beautiful area with blooming wildflowers and crystal clear water. I could see why it was a popular make-out spot.

"Wow, the tourist brochure really doesn't do this place justice. It's beautiful." Nate mused, as his eyes traversed over the area before turning to face us all. "Right, is everyone clear on the plan?"

"Look around and try to sense some raw magic, right? Really, really powerful ward-breaking raw magic..." I tried to sound confident but found myself wavering the more I thought about the situation.

"That's pretty much it. We'll split up and check over the area. Marcus and I will check up the path to the top of the Falls, you and Erich check down here."

"You sure? I could fly straight up there, it's no problem."

"Exactly, you'll be able to reach us faster if we find

anything up there and shout down to you. Plus, we can always just jump down into the pool if we need to get to you, it looks like fun."

I narrowed my eyes at him. "You're making sense, but are you sure this isn't just a tourist trip for you?"

He gasped, clutching at imaginary-pearls. "I would never! And I definitely didn't check the brochures last night. Now, Erich, since you can't sense magic like the rest of us, look for signs of rituals that have taken place. Sometimes they leave scorch marks. Weird smells and sulfur are good ones to watch out for."

"Do you really think demons could be involved in this?" Marcus asked.

"It's unlikely, but I wouldn't rule it out for now. This is exactly the kind of shit they'd do to mess with humans. Everyone, just keep an open mind for now. Anything's possible, so let's be ready."

As Nate and Marcus hiked the worn path to the top of the Falls, Erich and I began our search in the glade. I glided over to the other side of the pool and started looking over the rocks and trees, checking for carvings or any evidence of rituals. I knew this was a popular place for witches to have their full moon rituals, but the next one wasn't due for another two weeks. Things looked normal to me. None of the plants looked disturbed and nothing felt different to previous visits.

I walked over to the Red Cedar tree standing at the edge of this side of the glade and placed my hands on the bark, reaching out to it with my magic.

"Hello, friend. Will you speak to me? I need to ask you a question." I spoke in the Old Language, feeling the connection to the tree solidifying with each word.

The tree's voice resonated inside my mind immediately.

It had a slow, croaky voice, like an elderly man who just woke up from a nap. *"Hello! It's been so long since I've spoken to a Sprite, it's good to see one of you again. Ask your question, dear, I'll do my best to answer."*

"I'm searching for magic that has interfered with the wards surrounding Moonlit Falls. Have you seen any strange rituals here recently?"

The tree hummed thoughtfully for a moment. *"No, I can't say that I have. Though I've seen youths going into the cave behind the water before. Try searching there, dear."*

Finally, a lead! *"Thank you, I will!"* I placed a quick spell of protection on the kind tree, just like the one I placed on Delwyth the other day after my magic had freaked out.

I quickly flew over to Erich, who was carefully inspecting a small circle of daisies on the ground. He waved me over enthusiastically. "Hey, come take a look at this!"

"Erich, I think those are just daisies." I squatted down and gently curled my hand around one, holding it in my hand without picking it from the soil. I heard a happy, almost squeaky, *"Hi there, miss!"* in my head. I looked up at Erich with a grin across my face.

"Yep, those daisies are innocent little blooms."

"Damn, I thought the circle was important for something magical. Just a weird pattern."

"Sorry, but the Cedar on the other side gave me a hint. Did you know there's a cave behind the water?"

Erich shook his head, and we moved to the edge of the waterfall pool to check for ourselves. I kneeled at the water's edge, looking down just to check there wasn't something obvious I was missing. There were a few small fish down there, even a frog swimming closer to the bank, but nothing out of the ordinary. I tilted my head and looked at the crashing water of the waterfall. I couldn't see any entrances in the water, so the cave had to be behind there.

Leaving my tote bag on the shore, I leaned out into the pool, trying to get a better look at the potential entrance, but it was hard to make anything out behind the water. As I focused, I felt Erich's hands pick me up by my waist. "There's an easier way to look, Aggy. Time for a swim!"

"Don't you dare!" I screamed as Erich threw me towards the center of the pool. His laughter echoed through the area, but quickly died down as he noticed me hovering above the water level, unamused. "That was rude."

Erich just shrugged as he wriggled out of his backpack, kicked off his shoes, and tugged off his t-shirt, revealing a deliciously toned body. He tossed it onto the ground and gave me a grin. "I'll admit, I forgot you could fly for a second. But let's try Plan B."

I opened my mouth to ask what Plan B was, but Erich soared towards me in a leap I hadn't expected. I let out another scream as his arms wrapped around me in mid-air and he dragged me down to the water with him, my wings unable to hold us both in the air.

We resurfaced quickly, and as much as I wanted to glare, Erich's laughter was infectious. I settled for splashing him in the face and laughed as he spluttered on the water. "You totally deserved that and you know it!"

Erich grinned. "Yeah, but it was worth it to see the look on your face! Come on, we can swim through to the cave."

I took a fleeting glance up at the top of the Falls, where I could see Nate and Marcus looking down at us, laughing. They must have been able to hear my screams from up there. I waved and motioned to the waterfall to show them where we were going, before taking a deep breath and following Erich through to the cave.

CHAPTER TWELVE

The word 'cave' didn't do justice to this space at all. It was a massive cavern behind the waterfall. Looking around, I couldn't believe it had taken me so long to find out about it. It was stunningly beautiful. The deep pool from outside continued inside a few yards before sloping upwards to the rocky shore.

My soaked dress clung to me as I followed Erich out of the water, making my slight curves more noticeable. I fluttered my wings to shake off the water, lightly showering Erich in the process. Gazing at his glistening bare torso was a gift, and I was jealous that he'd had the foresight to take his shirt off before dragging me into the pool outside. I supposed I could steal his dry shirt once we were done here.

The inside was dustier than I expected. I didn't think anyone had been here as recently as the Cedar outside had led me to believe. A beam of light shone down from above, but I couldn't see an opening. I wondered if Nate and Marcus would spot an entrance from where they were exploring above us and climb down.

A few old footprints were dotted across the floor, but they looked like they had mostly been blown away by a breeze flowing through the cave from somewhere, cooling the room and making me shiver in my damp clothes. The cavern walls had every kind of crystal I could think of growing out from between the stones. It was amazing, but very unnatural.

"I've never seen so many different kinds of crystals growing in one place like this." My voice echoed through the room. "How do you think it's possible?"

"As someone who's fresh in the ways of your world, I'm just gonna assume it's magic and try not to think about it too much."

I reached out with my magic, feeling the energy of the Earth pulse around me from the crystals and up through my bare feet. A particularly strong pulse was coming from about halfway up the walls in a small alcove near the rushing waterfall.

As I flew up for a closer look, I noticed the crystal was completely dark. It didn't even seem to shine in the light like the other crystals, even though the surface was smooth. I hovered my hands around the crystal, feeling the tingle of its energy in my palms, but didn't sense anything too out of the ordinary. It was a strange, powerful crystal, that much was obvious, but it didn't feel like its power had been tapped into recently, if ever.

I glided back down to where Erich waited and shook my head sadly. The crystal didn't feel like what we were looking for. Honestly, I still wasn't sure what we were searching for exactly, but I knew I'd feel it once we found it.

As we continued to search the cave, I noticed Erich kept looking over at me as if he was about to say something, and then changed his mind. Something was clearly bothering him, so I decided to give him a little nudge. "Something on your mind?"

He thought for a moment, then shook his head. "It's nothing."

"You sure?" I pushed a bit further. "I don't want you to feel like you can't talk to me anymore."

"It's just... Aggy, you lied to me for years. Well, no, you didn't lie. But you didn't tell me the truth. And I like to think I've taken this whole 'magic-is-real' thing pretty damn well."

"You really have."

"Thank you. But something still feels off, and I think it's knowing that you've never trusted me as long as we've known each other. I mean, I've told you so much about myself over the years. Hell, I'm pretty sure you know everything down to my blood type, and you couldn't trust me with the simple fact that you aren't *human*!"

I flinched at his raised voice, but had to admit that he did have a point. As much as I'd wanted to tell him so many times over the years, I never did. I'd always convinced myself not to say anything. But it had never been out of a lack of trust in him.

"Erich, I trust you. I always have. Everything I've ever told you has been true—"

Erich cut me off, shouting. "But you couldn't break the news that you're magic?!"

"Because I didn't want to ruin your life!" I yelled back, my voice cracking.

He paused, staring at me. "You really think this has ruined my life?"

Inhaling a shaky breath, I looked up into Erich's dark, pained eyes. "Hasn't it? I know this has changed your life forever, and I can't say if it's for the better. You can never go back to not knowing about magic. You'll always see it wherever you go, and I didn't want to do that to you. You deserve so much happiness. And, well, ignorance is bliss and all that."

"Right. But you see, I'd rather have you in my life instead of blind joy without you. I've loved you for so long, and it hurts to discover all of this, only to find out that you never intended to tell me. You were always going to keep me away from you because you thought you knew what was best for me."

"You love me?" I squeaked.

"Of course that's the part you heard." Erich let out a wry chuckle. "Yeah, I've been in love with you since you recommended putting wildflower posies on my Grammy's grave. She could never decide on her favorite flower, but they were perfect for her. You even showed me the best place to pick them myself and helped me tie them in that fancy bow you do."

I remembered that. It felt so recent, but it was a little over two years ago now. We had sat at the gravesite for hours after the funeral, just talking to each other about anything until the sun finally set.

"I wanted to tell you so many times. But you're right, I thought I knew what was best." I rubbed my eyes with the heel of my hand as I held back tears, my shoulders shaking. "I just didn't want to take the risk that you would reject me and then be stuck seeing magic forever. Then we would have both been miserable."

Erich stepped towards me, closing the gap between us as he cupped my jaw in both his hands and kissed me fiercely. This was different to the quick kiss in Moonlit Magicks. This felt like he was calling my heart back from the edge of fear and giving it a safe, warm home with him.

"There's no way I would have ever rejected you." He spoke softly, running a hand through my damp hair before returning it to my face. "Even right now, when I want to be mad at you, I'm so damn happy there's nothing else standing in the way of us. I really don't know what this whole mate-spell-bonding-thing means, but I think it's given us a chance. And I want to take that chance with you."

"You seriously want to be with me the way I am? I don't even know what to do about the bond with Nate and Marcus."

His thumbs brushed over my cheeks as the tears I had been holding back finally fell. Waves of emotion poured out of me, and I couldn't tell if it was fear of the unknown or the joy of acceptance filling my heart.

"Listen to me, Aggy. I want you, even if you come as a magical package deal with them. I'm being open-minded, like Nate said. We can take this a day at a time and figure things out. All that matters is that we're safe and happy. Just promise me, no more secrets, okay?"

I nodded, grinning, with my face still cupped in Erich's hands. This was a better outcome than I'd ever hoped for. "No secrets. I want to take this chance too."

Our lips met again as I wrapped my arms around Erich's neck, pulling him closer and pressing my body to his. His hands moved from my face to my hips, hooking under my thighs and lifting me so I could wrap my legs around his waist securely.

Erich's tongue delved into my mouth, exploring and tasting every inch, leaving me breathless. His kisses moved to the corner of my mouth, across my jaw, and down my neck as he gripped the cheeks of my ass, massaging slowly. One of my hands ran through his closely cropped hair, and I felt him let out a soft moan into my neck. Soft kisses turned into nibbles going back up my throat, and I quickly realized that Erich's playful side extended into the bedroom. Or, in this case, into the secret waterfall cave.

Erich chuckled in my ear. "You taste like a river, Aggy."

"And whose fault is that?" I scoffed.

"Definitely mine. No regrets." He sealed our lips back together and kneeled on the floor, resting back on his feet, letting me straddle him. Hands traced over my thighs as they peeled back my wet skirt and pulled me closer by my hips. His growing hardness tented under his cargo shorts, encouraging me to grind my hips down and feel that delicious friction.

I leaned back slightly in Erich's embrace as he kissed down my chest, pulling the neckline of my dress down to expose my breasts. My decision to skip wearing a bra today was clearly a good one as nothing lay in the way of Erich's hot mouth closing over a nipple, while his hand caressed and tweaked the other. A throaty gasp left me as I heard splashes from the pool we'd entered from.

"Oh! Okay. Just came to check on you. I'm just gonna go ahead and assume you didn't find anything down here." Marcus paused while emerging from the pool. His amber eyes narrowed in annoyance, and a forced smile slashed across his face. "Do you guys need anything? Lube? A condom? Extra set of hands?"

My cheeks burned a bright red while Erich's hands continued toying with my breasts, seemingly unbothered by our audience of one. As Marcus's gaze remained fixated on what Erich was doing to me, my panties dampened and I couldn't help but grind down again. My thighs clenched in a growing need for more contact.

"We're good, thanks. We'll meet you outside when we're done!" Erich's casual response took me by surprise, but I couldn't worry about it as my brain focused on the steady movement of Erich's hips rising to meet my own.

"Guess I'll leave you to it. You better take care of her." A splash from the pool and Erich's chuckle were the only way I knew Marcus had left as my eyes were half-lidded in pleasure. His shifter nature must have been screaming at him to stop this and take control of the situation.

"Erich, we should go back. They're waiting for us." I tried to sound convincing, but the breathy moans escaping me meant my weak attempt fell on deaf ears.

"Let them wait. It sounds like I'm gonna be seeing a lot of these guys in my future and they need to know that you're my priority, not them."

"But the wards-"

"Can wait," he interrupted, trying to reassure me.

Any further protests I had were silenced by Erich's mouth covering my own. He gently flicked his tongue against my lips, encouraging me to open up for him. Our tongues danced together as one of Erich's hands pulled down the zipper at the back of my dress, letting it pool around my waist.

Pulling away, I stood in front of him in nothing but my panties and kicked the damp dress to one side. His gaze traversed over my body as he palmed his hand over the bulge in his cargo shorts. I straddled his lap again, grinding my hips down on his and running my hands down his chest, grateful for his lack of shirt.

Erich wrapped a strong arm around my waist, lifting me from the friction my body craved, and ran his fingers along the underside of my panties before pulling them aside and massaging my wet folds, coating his fingers. I couldn't hold back the moan that burst from me as he teased over my clit and slowly moved down, pushing a finger inside me.

His left hand moved back to my breast and his kisses slowly traveled across my jaw to a sensitive spot behind my ear, while my own hands struggled to unbutton his shorts. My mind was getting more frazzled with each curl of his fingers inside me, and my coordination was starting to suffer.

As soon as I finally got them loose and pushed down his boxers, I wrapped my hand around the base of his cock. A drop of pre-cum had beaded at the head and my thumb swiped over it, sliding my hand down his shaft and causing Erich to groan softly in my ear.

As my hips moved, riding his hand, I looked directly into Erich's dark eyes and spoke softly. "I want you to fuck me, Erich."

"I've waited so long to hear you say that." Erich removed his fingers from me, slick with my juices, and tugged my panties down my thighs. I moved to one side to get them off completely as Erich removed his own clothing, quickly grabbing a soaked wallet from a pocket in his shorts and pulling out a condom. He really was always prepared.

Kneeling over me, Erich asked, "Will the ground hurt your wings?"

I gave his shoulders a gentle push and guided him so I was back on top. "You're sweet to ask that, so I'll go easy on you."

Erich matched my grin and gave me a quick kiss while rolling the condom on. "Wow, so kind of you."

Hands held my hips, and I slowly lowered myself onto Erich's thick cock, taking deep breaths as his girth stretched me perfectly. I grasped his shoulders, digging my short nails in, as he filled me inch by delicious inch, until I was fully seated on his lap. He gently planted soft kisses to my forehead and cheeks while I adjusted to the feeling of him so deep inside me.

As I relaxed into the sensations flooding me, I began to steadily rock my hips and build up a rhythm that had me moaning and wanting more. Erich's hips rose to meet mine on their descent, and the sounds of our skin slapping together filled the cavern. He leaned his body up so our faces met and tongues tangled in our frantic movements. One hand twisted in my hair—not hurting, but still holding firmly—while the other caressed over my sensitive skin, down towards my aching clit.

Heat filled my belly and my wings twitched as I edged closer to my peak. Burying my face in the crook of Erich's neck, the combined scent of lavender and sweat enveloped me. The hand in my hair moved behind him to steady us as Erich's movements picked up in pace and his thrusts deepened.

"I want to feel you come, Aggy. Come for me now, all over my dick."

"Yes! Erich, I'm coming!"

His words tipped me over the edge, and I cried out in release as my body shook. My muscles tightened around his cock as waves of pleasure crashed over me, and I pulled Erich over the edge to his own bliss.

We collapsed back on the cave floor with our limbs entwined, sweat coating our bodies, and my head on Erich's chest, listening to the thumping of his heart. His arms wrapped around me securely, gently stroking one of my still-twitching wings, and my heart swelled with joy.

He didn't care what I was, so long as I was me.

CHAPTER THIRTEEN

Swimming out of the cave was a lot more refreshing than swimming in. I appreciated the quick chance to rinse the sweat and dirt off my body, even though it meant re-soaking my dress.

We climbed out of the water near our bags and Erich's shoes. I found Nate lying on the grass checking his phone with Marcus resting his head on his stomach, enjoying the afternoon sun shining down on them.

They both looked a little more rumpled than when I last saw them and I wondered what they'd been doing out here. Marcus's clothes looked like they'd dried out from the sun since his quick visit to the cave to check on us. It was cute to see them relaxing together like this. The past two days had been so stressful, the only times I'd seen them together they'd either been bickering or frantically problem solving. It made me wonder what a normal day would be like with them.

"Hey, Flower-Power, your headlights are on." Marcus made a wiggling motion at his nipples. I looked down and realized my own nipples were poking out under my wet dress. Wonderful.

I started squeezing the water out of the bottom of my dress, trying not to pout in envy as Erich put his dry t-shirt on. "I'm guessing you two didn't find anything either?" I made it a question, hoping to be wrong so things could go back to normal. Well, normal for Moonlit Falls at least.

"Nope. There were some interesting power levels, but nothing new or unstable." Nate spoke as he sat up, forcing Marcus to move as well.

"Yeah, this trip was a bust. What do we do now?" Marcus grumbled, slowly moving to his feet.

"I wouldn't say it was a total waste of time." Erich gave me a coy smile, and I felt my cheeks redden. We may not have found the answer to the wards problem, but it had definitely been worth the visit.

"Well, you would say that, wouldn't you?" Marcus smirked in Erich's direction as even the delicate points of my ears turned scarlet. Having Marcus walk in on us hadn't been ideal, but I couldn't deny that the attraction had intensified with him watching for those brief moments. Maybe there really was something to this mate bond, after all. "Though you didn't take all that long in there. I hope you were thorough—"

"U-Um... We should really plan our next move," I interrupted before Marcus could verbally dig us deeper into a hole. I wondered if he told Nate what he'd seen. "What else could be messing with the town wards?"

Silence descended as we took a moment to think. The town was named Moonlit Falls. It had made sense for the biggest of the Falls to have an intense amount of natural magical energy with a link to the town's wards. We were half right. There had been plenty of magical energy around the area, but nothing felt like it would mess up the wards so randomly, and there'd been no sign of any recent rituals.

"What about your tree?" Erich spoke up. "The one in the Village Green? It's super old and natural. Could it have the same magic stuff as the waterfalls?"

I couldn't believe I hadn't thought of it before. Delwyth was definitely older than the town, possibly even as old as the Falls themselves. It made perfect sense that she would be a source of natural magic. "Yes, Erich! That's it!"

"Not the first time she's said that today," Marcus muttered, but I did my best to ignore him.

"We need to get to the oak tree in the Village Green. I've always felt something incredible within Delwyth, so maybe this is..." I trailed off as realization hit me like a truck.

If Delwyth really was connected to the random drops in the wards, was I to blame? The timing was so close to that accident at the site with Marcus. But we'd checked Delwyth over and she was fine. Wasn't she?

"I need to go home first. I have to talk to Maeve, now."

"Would a phone call do?" Nate asked. "We should get to the Village Green as soon as we can. Bailey's been texting me updates, and things are getting crazy in town. Stone has the cops doing damage control all over town, and apparently Gunner was turned into a toad outside Bannock Bakery. Jasper had to move fast before a human reporter got a picture of the poor guy. It looks like he doesn't remember now, but he got close to having actual evidence of supes."

Damn, it sounded like the sightings were getting more frequent. We wouldn't be able to stay hidden much longer if things kept up like this.

"No, I need to talk to her in person. We can take the other trail, the one on the Eastern side of the river, it'll go straight past my house on the way back to town. We'll hardly lose any time at the house if we hurry."

The guys looked unconvinced, so I pushed a little more. I hoped that using my cutest big-eyes and not-quite-begging voice would work on them, while hiding my own worry. "Please, this is really important."

Their eyes softened—even Marcus's—and I mentally cheered for myself. Big-eyes won again!

We crossed the river quickly, with them jumping between rocks while I flew next to them to keep them steady, then followed the well-used trail back towards town. This trail was favored by tourists for its more direct route between the town and Cupid Falls, while still being a beautiful hike. I often saw Laz walking her husky, Kyrian, along this trail.

Dashing between the trees, we made good time coming down alongside the river. There was no conversation this time, as everyone seemed to sense the urgency much more now. I glanced behind me to see the guys following closely and led them down a side path to the glen hiding the Fae Community.

"Where's your house? I thought you lived around here..." Erich looked around until he spotted the familiar toadstool-shaped postbox standing next to the tree I called home. He'd visited more than a few times over the years for movie nights, but he knew the house as a well-built cabin. Not a literal tree with a door carved into the side. "Oh, you've gotta be kidding me."

Marcus sighed, massaging his temples with one hand. "I'm not even surprised at this point."

I made a ta-da motion at the front door. "Welcome to my house. As you can see, it's a tree. I will not be taking questions at this time, just take your shoes off when we go in. Maeve hates it when I track dirt into the house."

Before they could try to make any more sarcastic comments, I unlocked the door and hovered inside, moving straight through the living room to the door leading down to Maeve's bedroom in the basement.

Knocking loudly, I yelled to her. "Maeve! I need to talk to you!"

"Coming!" Her muffled yell sounded from behind the door before she pulled it open. "Wow, you look like shit. Did you fall in the river? You're soaked."

"Something like that. Talk to me in the bathroom while I clean up?"

She nodded, and we headed for the stairs. I was halfway up before I realized she had stopped, having noticed the guys in the living room. They were fanned out. Erich sat comfortably on the couch, while Nate admired the decorative wooden lovespoons hanging on the wall, and Marcus inspected the many houseplants placed around the room.

Maeve flashed a pleading glance at me as she looked them over. "Please don't tell me your new collection of walking, talking dildos are already moving in. Wait, wait. Not you, Erich. You're cool, you deliver my stuff."

Erich gave her a satisfied grin as Nate stood there in shock, not sure whether to be offended by Maeve's comments or not.

Marcus just smirked, moving towards us. "Let me guess, this is where you give us the 'if you ever hurt her' speech, right?"

"Oh no, my sweet summer child. No. Aggy does not need me to defend her. She looks innocent enough, but if you *do* ever hurt her, make her cry, or fuck up in any way, she's going to end you just fine all on her own. I'll just be there to help move your body." Maeve gave him a terrifyingly sweet smile and petted his cheek like a puppy. It was nice that she had so much confidence in me.

Pulling her by the arm before an actual fight could break out, I dragged Maeve up to the bathroom and swung my legs over the side of the bathtub to start cleaning off the lingering dirt.

"Close the door? I think I've fucked up."

"As much as that explains the state of your hair and your dress, I'm gonna need you to be more specific. Did you not find anything at the Falls?"

I shook my head. "I mean, I found a hell of an orgasm behind a waterfall, but that was just a fun surprise. I think my magic hurt Delwyth last week, and she might be linked to the wards somehow."

"Are you sure? I didn't sense anything wrong with her physically when I checked her over for you. You even put that protection spell on her, right?"

"Yeah, but I feel like this is all my fault. You're sure you didn't sense anything?"

My hopeful question was answered with a sad smile. "Positive. But maybe this is something you should call your mom about. She would probably know what to look for if Delwyth really is connected like you think she is."

"No. No way." I shut her down quickly. "*Mam* would just use this as an excuse to get me to go back home. I can't call her."

Maeve sighed, passing me a towel for my legs as I pivoted around on the edge of the tub to stand up. "What can I do to help?"

"I don't really know. We're going to go to the Village

Green now. Hopefully I'll sense something, but I don't even really know what I'm looking for."

"You'll know it when you feel it. Go put some clean clothes on. I'll distract your guys. And think about calling your mom. She's a shit sometimes, but she knows her shit."

"You have such a way with words."

Following Maeve out of the bathroom, I quickly went up the next flight of stairs to my bedroom to find Marcus lounging across my bed, propped up by my many cushions.

"Nice place you have here, Sunshine."

"What are you doing in my room?" I asked, tiredness leaking through my voice.

"I wanted to talk to you. C'mon, let's go outside." Rolling off the bed with the smooth grace only a snake could achieve, Marcus took me by the hand and led me to my open window. For some reason, I didn't mind his touch. Maybe I was more exhausted than I thought. Or maybe he was just wearing me down.

"We can't take the stairs?"

"We could, but this is much more fun." He grinned as he climbed out onto a thick branch and jumped down to the forest floor, his shifter agility helping him land with ease.

I glided down after him, my curiosity winning over my desire to crawl into bed and emotionally recharge. "Okay, so what's going on? Why are we out here?"

"We're out here because you need to be calm and focused. Touch the Earth and soil and shit, right?"

My surprise must have shown on my face, because he gave me a reassuring smile as he walked me away from the house a bit, towards the riverside. We stopped near the edge and sat on the grass.

"You dig your toes in the ground when you're stressed,

and I overheard the conversation with your roommate. I thought coming out here might help."

"I don't know if you're sweet or creepy right now."

"Can't I be both?" He grinned, but it faded quickly as his expression turned serious. "I'm sorry. I was curious and shouldn't have eavesdropped. But I'm glad I did, because I think you need this more than you're going to admit."

He had a point there. Closing my eyes, I lay back against the ground and spread my fingers, gently brushing over the grass. As I focused on the ground at my back, I felt my magic pull from the Earth and fill me up. It was a strange sensation, like taking that first sip of cool water on a hot day.

My eyes opened to see Marcus resting back on his elbows, watching me curiously. "You okay now?"

"I am. You were right, I needed this. I'm just so scared that if all this is my fault—"

"Then we'll deal with it." He interrupted me. "Try not to worry about something until there's actually something to worry about. And if it turns out you're right and we need to call your mom for some tree-advice, we'll help you through it."

"Thanks, but you don't know my mother."

Marcus moved to lie next to me. Our shoulders brushed each other as he scooched in closely. "That's true, but I do happen to know a thing or two about parents thinking less of their kids. Nate's family likes me, they're good people, but my own parents are a very different story."

I turned on to my side, facing him as he stared up at the sky. There was still so little I knew about him, but every moment I was becoming more comfortable next to him. "Will you tell me that story?"

He turned his head to look at me. Our faces were close

enough that we almost shared the same breath. Our fingers tangled together between us, both of us seeking that small comfort from the other. "Eventually, yeah. I never really thought I'd get a fated mate after the bond with Nate happened. But when I thought about it, I never planned on keeping secrets from that person. So, lucky you, you'll get to know all the juicy details if you decide you want what comes with them."

"I guess we'll find out soon, then. For now, I don't want to rush into agreeing to things, especially a bond like this."

His free hand stroked along my jaw, making my heart pound in my chest. "Smart little Sprite. But just in case I can tempt you into taking this chance..." He trailed off as he leaned forward and kissed me.

This time, I didn't hesitate. I wanted to taste him and know what I would be getting into, or know what I would be missing out on. His kiss was different from Erich's and Nate's. Each press of his lips and tease of his tongue felt like it was claiming me, seducing me a bit further, to the point where all I wanted was more.

Eventually, I pulled away, my face flushed and breathless. "Definitely tempting," I conceded.

His grin was back, and he smooched my lips once more. "Perfect. Ready to go back in?"

I nodded, finally feeling the confidence I needed. If I really was the reason Moonlit Falls was in trouble, I was ready to do whatever I had to do to fix it.

CHAPTER FOURTEEN

Once I'd changed into some clean work clothes and had a quick good-luck-*cwtch* from Maeve, we piled out of the house and headed into town. It wasn't a long walk, but along the way, I noticed Nate giving me a little smile. I knew that he'd seen me coming back into the house with Marcus, but I think it really did make him happy to see us bonding a bit.

As we neared the edge of town and the footpath turned into a road, Nate stopped me with a hand on my shoulder. "Aggy, I just thought, we're going to have to cover up your wings. Getting through the whole town with messed-up wards is just asking for trouble from the humans."

I cringed. "Could you just crowd around me? I'm pretty small."

Nathaniel shook his head. "We need to play it safer than that. Marcus, can you lose your overshirt and see if it'll hide the wings?"

Marcus quickly tugged off his long-sleeved flannel shirt, not bothering to undo the buttons, revealing a plain gray t-shirt underneath.

"I really don't think this is going to work."

"Well, it won't with that attitude. Now, arms up," Marcus scolded me as he forced my arms into his shirt. The problem was, every time we tried to lower the shirt to lie flat across my back, my wings fluttered involuntarily and lifted me a foot off the ground before someone caught me.

"Got her." Nathaniel held me by the shoulders, keeping my bare feet on the ground.

"It's not my fault! My wings hate being bound down, even my winter clothes have slits in the back to let them out." I let out an exasperated sigh as my wings beat in frustration.

Nathaniel gave me a comforting smile as Marcus tried to wrestle the shirt down behind me, cursing as one of my wings hit him square in the face. "I know it's not your style, but you're the one who looks the least human. You already stand out for not wearing shoes, so we can't risk your wings being seen as well. Marcus is gonna cover his snake-eyes with sunglasses so you're not alone in this."

"Oh, he's going to wear sunglasses? What a hero! Generations will sing of his sacrifice, I'm sure."

"Watch it, Flower Power," Marcus growled behind me, and I flipped him the bird.

"It just feels so wrong to me. I never have trouble sleeping on my wings or wrapping up in a duvet, but covering them outside like this... it's all wrong."

"Well, we don't have time to go to Moonlit Magicks for one of Bailey's glamor spells, so this will have to do. Fate of the town and all that. Now just hold still..." Marcus pulled at the shirt again and tied it tightly around my waist. "Hah! There! Totally human." He stepped back as I checked his DIY wing-tuck in a nearby car window.

I glared at Marcus. "You've turned me into Quasimodo!"

Marcus rolled his eyes. "It's not that bad, right, Erich?"

I swung my glare towards Erich, who stifled a laugh. "It's, um... It's a look."

"It'll have to do. Come on. We need to get to your tree before a human notices the minotaur working behind the bar at Nessie's." Nate handed Marcus a pair of sunglasses from his backpack and led us into town.

The sun was just starting to set, but there were a surprising number of people around. The nightlife in Moonlit Falls was busy thanks to the underground nightclub, Flare, and Nessie's Pub, but hopefully Maeve got the word out in time for the vampires to take the night off.

We shuffled through town, with Erich staying close at my back to cover me in case I suffered the wing equivalent of a nip-slip.

"You're sure this tree is the conduit we're looking for?" Nate asked.

"Well, it's the only thing that makes sense. The Falls were powerful, sure, but they're too far from the center of town to be what powers the cloaking spell. Delwyth is the next oldest landmark, so she's our best bet." I didn't mention my magic blast from last week. Hopefully that didn't have an effect, but we were going to find out soon enough, anyway.

Marcus chuckled, looking at me from behind his sunglasses. "I still can't believe you named the tree. I mean, I can, it's a very you thing to do, but that name really doesn't roll off the tongue. Should've gone with something easy, like Spruce Willis."

Erich barked out a laugh, and Nate snorted into his hand. I did my best to keep my eyes from rolling, but it didn't go well. "You're making fun of the mystical tree that's likely our only hope?"

"I'm not *making* fun. I'm just saying that names should *be* more fun. Oh, oh! Donald Trunk!" Marcus grinned, clearly proud of himself.

Nate shook his head. "Oh no, definitely not."

I sighed in relief, glad to have someone on my side. "Thank you."

"Keanu Leaves." Nate received a swift high-five from his familiar for that one.

"Yes! Ooh, what about Tony Bark? Tree-yoncé?" Marcus looked almost giddy while coming up with ideas.

Nate's laugh echoed through the street. "Or Chris Pine? Nah, too simple."

"Stop it! Besides, Delwyth is a 'she'," I scoffed.

There was a long pause. I thought that the conversation was finally over, until Erich—who had been quiet up to now—spoke two simple words.

"Queen LaTree-fa."

Marcus audibly gasped and held his hand over his heart. He stalked over to Erich, squishing me between them as he held Erich's face in both hands and leaned in. "I'm keeping you."

I slapped Marcus's chest a few times until he backed off, chuckling to himself. "You know I mean no real disrespect, Sweetheart. You named the tree. It's adorable."

"I didn't name her, she named herself. And honestly, I hope she drops a bloody branch on you."

"Fighting words, m'dear. Careful now."

"You're much more attractive when you're quiet, Danger Noodle."

"Ooh, I love it when you say I'm hot. Maybe later we could—"

"Stop, both of you," Nate interrupted Marcus's retort as we finally approached the Village Green. "We're here. Let's see if Delwyth has some answers for us."

"She's always been so quiet before, I don't know what's going to make today any different," I mused as we walked onto my renovation site. The grass was growing well, thanks to the sprinkles of magic I'd added, and it already looked so much better than when I first started. I'd be able to start placing the foliage and furniture soon if everything went to plan now. But that was a huge "if".

The guys fanned out around me as I approached Delwyth slowly, looking from her roots all the way up to the tips of her branches in her canopy. She was magnificent. I carefully stepped around one of her large roots and kneeled in the grass, placing my hands on her bark. Keeping more of my body in contact with the Earth was helping me harness my magic, so I closed my eyes and took a deep breath, taking that concentrated energy and focusing it on Delwyth.

"Hear me, Delwyth. Please hear me and speak to me..." I whispered the prayer and pushed my magic harder, my nails digging into the crevices of her trunk. My wings flexed almost painfully as my magic struggled to get through to Delwyth. A distant shout sounded in my head. My arms dropped to my side, and I fell back against the warm body holding me up.

Nate cradled my exhausted body to his chest, gently stroking my hair. "You're okay, Aggy, rest for a moment."

"Here, drink this." Erich passed over a bottle of water from one of the bags, and I took it in a shaking hand.

Drinking the water in a few big gulps, I pushed away from Nate and moved back to Delwyth. "I nearly got through to her. Let me try again."

"No way, Aggy, it's too much." Marcus pulled me back

by my shoulders, glaring up at Delwyth. "I don't know what the fuck this tree's problem is, but we'll figure out something else. There's gotta be another way that doesn't involve you hurting yourself like this."

Turning to face him, I reasoned, "I heard something before the connection severed, that's more than I've had from her in months. I just need to push through, and then I'll be able to talk to her. We'll get our answers."

Marcus's glare moved to me. I could feel his reluctance to let me attempt it again coming off him in waves. After a few seconds of tense silence, he sighed. "Nate, can you give her a magic boost? Like the ones you give Bailey and Ellis."

Nate scratched his neck, deep in thought. "I can try. My witch magic might not be as compatible with her Fae magic, but it's worked for Bailey before, and he's half-Fae. You up for it, Aggy?"

Offering him my hand, I gave him a firm nod. "Ready when you are."

Nate's brow furrowed in concentration as he took my hand and pulled out a blade much larger than the compact version he kept on his keys, then expertly swiped it across the meaty part of my palm. Doing my best not to flinch, I kept my eyes on Nate while he whispered a spell, pressing my bloody hand against Delwyth's bark.

My breath was sucked out of my lungs the moment the spell activated. I had to brace myself with my other hand to stay sitting upright. The shout I'd heard before rang through my ears, getting clearer and more distinctly female every second until it suddenly stopped and the only sound I could hear was my own pounding pulse.

Blinking slowly, I noticed a pale glow around Delwyth. It brightened in gentle waves, steadily gaining momentum, until the light began to shape itself into the ghostly visage of an elderly woman standing next to me.

"Delwyth?"

The female figure looked at me with glowing—yet unfocused—eyes and nodded slowly. *"It's good to finally speak to you, Agate."*

Incredible. I'd only ever heard of a few Sprites who had ever seen a Tree Spirit before. The magic it would normally take is far beyond what I possessed, not to mention the spirit needs to be willing to show themselves. Tree spirits, while usually talkative, never seem to feel the need to show themselves. When I asked my mother about it years ago, she described it as a sort of last resort for them to be heard, but it was dependent on someone with the right magic being around to see them.

Finally seeing her now, I couldn't help but notice how weak and frail she appeared. She wore a long white dress. It was well-worn and drooped over her bony frame. Her shoulders were hunched over as she clutched at her chest, like each beat of her heart was painful for her. If this was the visual manifestation of Delwyth's magical essence that I was seeing, she really was in trouble.

"You're so hurt... Oh no, I was right. This is all my fault." Painful tears welled up in my eyes until I felt the palm of her hand cupping my jaw, guiding my eyes to hers. The sensation of her hand was strange, like a tingling that wasn't quite real, but I knew she was there.

"Listen to me, Agate. You were a catalyst, yes, but not the cause of my injuries. Now, I need your help, little Sprite."

"*What can I do?*" My trembling voice squeaked as Erich's hand gently stroked small, comforting circles at the small of my back.

Glancing at the guys, it was clear by their confused

expressions that they couldn't see Delwyth's spiritual form at all. As far as they were concerned, their mate was just crying at a tree. Which, I suppose, was technically true, but they couldn't see how impressive I was actually being. Give a Sprite some credit.

"There is a spell anchored to me, one that has been used by the Paranormal Council for decades to lower the wards hiding supernaturals in town each year on Samhain. It was meant to be used for loved ones on the other side of the veil to be able to visit their human families, without the danger of exposing the community at large."

I nodded my head as I followed her explanation. I wasn't looking forward to Marcus's smug "I told you so" when I relayed this information. He definitely called it back in Moonlit Magicks yesterday.

"But the spell should have only stayed with me that night. When it automatically worked again the following year, the council should have removed it, but they merely celebrated their good fortunes. Even now, in this generation, they have never thought to check on the consistency of the spell. Each year it grew as it ate away at my magic. It's killing me, Agate, and I can't hold it back anymore."

My bleeding hand shook as I clung to Delwyth's bark. Rage boiled inside me, thinking of every carefree night of fun the residents had each Halloween, without knowing what it had been costing them each year. *"Tell me how I can help you, Delwyth. How can I remove the spell?"*

"Little Sprite, it cannot be removed from me now. It has been too long."

I jumped to my feet, barely remembering to keep contact with the trunk. *"No! I can't accept that! You've been part of this town from the beginning, and we... I need you here."*

Delwyth smiled down at me, her pale, ghostly wrinkles creasing around her shining eyes. *"You're sweet, little Sprite. But the council members who cast this spell were careless fools. They never stopped to consider the burden they were placing upon me. Agate, I've watched this town grow over many centuries, and I will not allow irrevocable damage to be done to this wonderful town."*

Erich's hands moved to my hips as I swayed unsteadily on my feet. I wasn't bleeding much—there was no chance of blood loss—but my head was spinning, and my vision was beginning to blur. Even with Nate's boost, I was using too much magic holding this connection.

"Remove me from the ground, Agate, and the spell will be removed with me.

"But you wouldn't survive. I-I couldn't..."

"You will. Or this town will never be safe again."

At her words, my hand slipped from her bark and I collapsed. A blur of voices shouted out my name, but darkness overcame me before I could even hit the ground.

CHAPTER FIFTEEN

When I finally woke up, my cheek was smushed up against a hard body. Slowly blinking open my eyes, my mind finally registered the toned arms curled around me, holding me still. The chest I was resting on rose and fell evenly, and I assumed whoever I was on top of was asleep. They smelled good, though: woodsy with the lingering remains of a cologne. I was reluctant to try to pull away. His arms were so cozy and safe.

As I shifted my head slightly to try to look around the room and figure out where I was—it definitely wasn't my house—something wet grazed my cheek. Uh-oh, I might have drooled on him. Time to move.

It felt impossible to pull away from the firm grip surrounding me, so I settled for shimmying down the body beneath me until I was free. Luckily my wings were already below his arms. As my face reached some wonderfully toned abs, I heard chuckling from above me. I froze, silently praying this man's vision was based on movement.

"Good to see you're feeling better. Are you having fun down there, Sunshine?"

What were the chances of the ground opening to swallow me whole? Usually quite high, with my brand of magic, but I sensed we were at least one story above the ground, ruining my escape plan.

"It's pretty cozy here, not gonna lie."

Marcus peeled back the covers over my head, smirking down at where my head lay on his abdomen. "Y'know, if you wanna shuffle down just a little farther, we could have some fun—Hey!"

I silenced his suggestion with a quick slap on his exposed chest, hitting him right on a nipple. "Nope! Bad Danger-Noodle!"

Before I knew what was happening, Marcus had flipped us over and pinned me down to the mattress. His hips dug into my own as he leered at me. My heart pounded against my chest as his mouth brushed over my cheek to my whisper in my ear.

"Hmm, judging by this reaction, I think you're curious as to just how dangerous I can be. Isn't that right, Agate?"

No nickname. I was in trouble. I couldn't even deny what he'd said. Even without his whispers, just looking up at him this closely had my cheeks flushing red, and I had to remind my hips not to rub up against his. I didn't know if this was the mate bond, but frankly, it was time to stop giving a damn.

Giving in, I turned my head to the side and met his lips with my own in a fervor Marcus easily matched. His mouth devoured me, licking and nipping at my lips, barely giving me an opportunity to take a breath before diving back in and making my brain forget all thoughts and cares.

"Oh, hey, you're awake!" Erich's voice chirped from the bedroom door. "We were getting worried. How do you feel?"

Marcus curled around me, growling into the curve of my neck. "She's fine. We're busy."

Clearing my throat awkwardly, I gently nudged Marcus's shoulder in a motion to let me up. "Actually, I could really use the bathroom."

"That's fair. You've been asleep for just over a day," Erich explained.

My jaw dropped. "Seriously?! What time is it?"

Marcus rolled away from me, looking defeated, with one arm flopped over his eyes. "Nearly eight? I dunno, I was too busy enjoying our nap and other activities before we were interrupted."

"Yeah, payback's a bitch, isn't it?" Erich deadpanned.

I tried not to giggle at their banter, but I couldn't help letting out a small laugh. It was nice to see them getting along, even if it was sort of at my expense. "Uh, where's the bathroom? And where are we?"

Sitting up and stretching out his arms, Marcus answered, "Ellis and Bailey's house. Me and Nate have rooms here while their other roommates are out of town. Bathroom's down the hall on the right, need an escort?"

"I think I'll manage by myself." I leaned in to give him a quick kiss; because despite being glad for the break to go pee, I had been enjoying our make-out session. But I was quickly pulled onto his lap with both of his hands cupping my ass as he reminded me just what I'd be missing out on.

"Come downstairs when you're done. You must be hungry." With a swift tap on my butt, Marcus sent me on my way to the bathroom. The moment I sat on the toilet, I really could tell that it had been a whole day, I had been nearly bursting.

While splashing some water on my face and cleaning out the remnants of dirt from my fingernails, I noticed that someone must have cleaned my feet before putting me to bed. I wasn't sure if that was sweet or obsessive, but it was definitely appreciated.

I made my way downstairs, following the delicious scent of cooking onions and garlic wafting from the kitchen. I found Nate stirring something while Marcus cut up some vegetables. Nate looked up from the stove, and I could feel the sense of relief radiating from him.

"Good to see you on your feet, Aggy. Are you hungry? We're making a quick stir-fry, since it's getting late, with a veggie option for you."

"Dinner for breakfast. It's like brinner in reverse. I like it." I took a seat at the breakfast bar, watching them. "So what happened after I passed out?"

Erich took a seat next to me and passed me a glass of water, which I chugged down in record time. I hadn't realized how empty my stomach was until now.

"You didn't miss much. If anything, we were gonna ask *you* what happened."

Marcus leaned against the counter, done with his cooking duties for now. "Yeah, all we could see was a one-sided argument with a tree in a language that sounded a lot like a sneeze."

That sounded about right.

Erich continued, "All we could do was check you weren't hurt and look after you the best we could. We didn't have to do much. Most of the time Scales wouldn't let go of you long enough for Nate and me to get close." He gestured to Marcus, who avoided eye-contact with me for once. I had to bite my lip to stop myself laughing at the nickname.

It was sweet, really. I knew that shifters got protective over their mates, but I'd never seen it firsthand. Though after waking up in a cocoon of his arms, I guess I could say I'd experienced it now.

Nate looked over from the stove, grinning. "It was pretty adorable, he watched over you all day while we went to work and sent us text updates. He even made a group chat!"

"Shut up! It's not like I was needed in the shop today, and someone had to keep an eye on Tinkerbell," Marcus growled.

"Wait, going back a second. What do you do in the shop? You're not a witch and you don't do magic, so..." I trailed off, confused.

Marcus rolled his eyes, as if I was stupid for asking. "I'm an accountant. I do stuff behind the scenes."

"Wait, like one of those sexy accountants from Screech? You know, 'accountants'." I made the finger quotes in the air, wiggling my eyebrows a little.

If Marcus rolled his eyes back any farther, they'd do a flip inside his skull. His jaw twitched as he mentally searched for more polite words than he clearly wanted to say.

"No. Not like them. I work with numbers. I like them. They're predictable and make sense. Can we change the subject now!?"

I bit my lower lip to keep from giggling. It was fun seeing a different side to everyone. Maybe a life with them as mates would be fun after all.

"Thank you for looking after me. I'd never used so much magic at once, and I guess my body couldn't take it. I feel okay now, though." I smiled, trying to reassure them all, but quickly got distracted by Nate putting a bowl of stir-fried rice and veggies in front of me.

"You can thank us by eating up and telling us what Delwyth told you. Judging from your tone—even in the sneezy-language—it didn't sound good."

"'Sneezy language'? Really? I thought you were the good one."

Nate gave the top of my head a gentle kiss and took a seat opposite me, with Marcus beside him. "Fooled you. Now eat up and give us the bad news."

I began to relay what Delwyth had told me between bites, doing my best to focus on the delicious flavors instead of the sense of impending doom. Unfortunately, the doom quickly infected the others, judging by their grim expressions. By the time I'd finished my explanation, my bowl was empty, and I was bracing myself for the full force of their reactions.

"Is there any other way of removing the spell without killing the tree?" Erich looked at me with sad puppy-eyes. He knew my love for Delwyth better than anyone at the table, even before he knew about magic.

"No, the spell is too deeply ingrained. Ironically, if I tried any of my healing spells on Delwyth now, I would only be giving it more to feed on. The disruptions to the wards would just spread faster until it covers the whole town."

"And all the Supernaturals in town would be permanently exposed," Nate muttered, finishing my grim conclusion. "We really don't have a choice here."

No one wanted to say it. None of them wanted to tell me to uproot Delwyth for the sake of the town, but the shadows lingering in their eyes said it for them.

"I think it's time you called your mom." Marcus's deep voice spoke softly. "Hopefully, it turns out we're missing something and she can help."

I scratched my neck absentmindedly as I sighed. "Yeah, but I hate it when you're right."

"It happens a lot, you'll get used to it. Speaking of, are you gonna tell your mom about us?" The caring tone in his voice was quickly replaced with mischief, making me roll my eyes. Despite looking annoyed, I was glad for him lightening the mood a bit. Even if it wasn't something I was ready to talk about yet.

"Look, I'm willing to see where this mate-thing goes. Let's just leave it at that for now, okay? My *mam* doesn't need to know anything more than the problem, right now."

As I left the room to Marcus cheering about the three of them not being considered the problem anymore, I mentally prepared myself to call my mother. Our last conversation had made me so emotional that my magic had lashed out, bringing all of this to our attention. I never enjoyed being mad at her. We just had trouble understanding each other sometimes. Hopefully, I was going to be able to stay in control this time.

Flopping down on the bed I'd woken up in, I pulled my phone out of my shorts' pocket and quickly texted Maeve to let her know I was okay, then dialed my mother.

After only a few rings, she answered. "Hello, Agate? This is a surprise. You don't normally call this late for you."

"Hiya, *Mam*." My voice immediately cracked as I spoke, and I cringed, hating what my nerves were doing to me.

"What's wrong, darling? You sound strange."

I took a deep breath and sat up on the bed. "*Mam*, hypothetically, if I magically damaged an ancient tree that's used to anchor a timed ward-exclusion spell, and then that spell began glitching all over town causing havoc with the humans, how would I go about fixing it?"

The phone was silent for a few moments, and I started

to wonder if she had just hung up on me in her disappointment.

Instead, she shocked me. "Are you okay?"

"I... I'm so scared," I admitted, before starting to babble. "This week has been crazy, and frustrating, and wonderful; and now I think I have to destroy my favorite part of town so I can save it. All this time I thought I was *protecting* Delwyth and keeping her safe and healthy. When actually she's been the one protecting all of us in town, while *I* gave power to the thing she's been holding back! What kind of fucked up logic is that?"

She took a moment to make sure I was done with my little rant before speaking. "I'll let the cursing slide today because you seem to need it. But you need to think carefully. Wards are a tricky business and ward-exclusions are even trickier. A spell on top of a spell rarely works out well for long. How long has this one been active?"

"She said it had been decades. The Samhain ball it's used for has been a tradition here for under a century for sure, probably around fifty years or so."

"So she's at her breaking point. Wait a moment, she finally spoke to you?"

I grinned through the sadness of the situation. She definitely hadn't seen that coming. "I didn't just speak to her, I *saw* her."

I practically preened when I heard my mother's proud gasp through the phone, and my own voice started to mirror her excitement. "It was incredible! Nate boosted my magic with one of his spells and I was able to actually *see* her spirit form as she talked to me."

"Who's Nate?"

Of course, that was the part she focused on. Being the

first Sprite to see a tree's spirit form in generations? Meh. Being near a man? Explain everything!

"That's not important right now. *Mam*, I really need your help to deal with this spell." I finally admitted it out loud, but didn't get any of the relief I thought I would. At least she didn't rub it in my face that I was asking her, though.

"Agate, there's a point with everything where the healthiest and safest thing for everyone involved is just to let go. Tell me, what did Delwyth tell you to do?"

"She said to remove her from the land to stop the spell."

"See? You already have your answer. Though it's quite adorable that you actually considered listening to me for a change."

Ignoring the snide comment, I stayed focused. "I just don't think I can do it, both emotionally and physically. I don't think I have it in me to destroy her."

"You could get Nate to help you once you've explained who he is."

"Subtle as a boulder, as always."

"Oh hush, child, I'm just showing interest." She huffed down the phone, and I could hear her wings thump at her back in frustration as she seemed to compose herself. "If you were able to physically witness the spirit form, you clearly have the power you need available to you. Harness it and do what you need to. Then come home for a visit with Nate. I know you're hiding something else and I'm curious."

She made it all sound so easy, but I could tell this was the best advice I was going to get from her without having to explain about Nate. That situation—including Erich and Marcus—was a call for another day.

"I'm hanging up now. *Diolch, Mam*."

"And don't forget to message your cousin, Kacy. She misses you! *Caru ti,* Agate!"

I smiled, genuinely feeling the familial warmth in my heart. "I love you, too."

CHAPTER SIXTEEN

A knock on the door pulled me out of my thoughts. I'd been lying on the bed since the call with my mother, replaying everything over in my head, though not as negatively as last week.

Mam believed I could do what Delwyth had told me to do, but doubt was still eating away at my mind. I was definitely going to need more than just a boost from Nate to completely remove something so large and powerful in its own right. My own power alone wasn't going to be enough.

"Hey, how'd it go?" Erich asked as he cracked the door open. Seeing me on the bed, he closed the door behind him and lay next to me, pulling me into a one-armed hug that I gladly snuggled into.

"It was okay, actually. Probably one of our better conversations. It only took the fate of a town for us to be civil to one another for more than six minutes."

"Huh. Go figure. Any advice for us?"

I shook my head. "She basically just told me to get on with it. There's no avoiding what I have to do. I just need to find a way to do it without passing out from getting drained again."

Erich's hand gently stroked up and down my arm as we lay there in silence for a few minutes. Eventually, he spoke. "I'm okay with it, you know."

I looked up at him, confused.

"Nate and Marcus, I mean. I'm okay with the mate-thing," he clarified. "I thought I'd be weirded out at the idea of you being with them, but they're good people. I was happy when you said you wanted to see where all this goes between the four of us."

"Thank you. I don't want to rush anything, but something about being around you all feels so right. I don't want to ignore that."

Turning on to his side to face me, he placed a soft kiss on my forehead. "Good. You should spend some time with them. We had a few years' head-start, after all. I just don't want you to worry about me in all this. Do what feels right to you, okay?"

"I will. Thank you, Erich." Resting my hand on his cheek, I kissed him softly, caressing his lips with my own to seal our sweet promise.

After a few moments, Erich mumbled against my mouth. "I need to go, Aggy. I'm sorry. Gramps and I originally had plans to go to the diner tonight, but I want to keep him home while the wards are acting crazy. We settled on a movie night instead, and I'm already super late. He's probably asleep, but I should be there just in case."

I smiled. He was too sweet. "No problem. Get going and tell him I said hi."

"I will. And don't even think of going to try anything with Delwyth. You still need some rest. Stay here and have a good night with the others."

A gentle blush colored my cheeks at that implication. I'd been planning to head home myself, but I supposed it was already late. Spending another night here made sense.

Reluctantly, we left the bed, and I watched Erich leave from the front door. When I returned to the kitchen, Nate and Marcus were finishing up cleaning the dishes. It was strange seeing them being so domestic for some reason. Marcus was the first to notice me hovering in the doorway and beckoned me in with a finger.

"Human gone home?" he asked.

"Yep. You should really stop calling him that, though."

"I'll have you know we talked about it, actually. Almost like we're adults or something, I dunno." He stuck his tongue out at me, contradicting his point perfectly, but still making me laugh. "I overheard your call, by the way. Not on purpose, though. Just, shifter hearing. We'll figure something out. Try not to worry for now."

"Easier said than done, but I'll try. Can we watch a movie or something? I'm too awake to try to sleep again so soon, and I need a distraction since I'm apparently housebound."

Nate smirked at me, sharing a mischievous look with Marcus. He threw the dish towel he was using onto the countertop and moved over to me. "I know exactly what'll help you relax."

He pulled me closer to him by my hips and lowered his mouth to mine. My lips opened, inviting him in, and his tongue glided over my own, coaxing a soft moan from my throat. Hands reached around from behind me, cupping my breasts through my shirt.

Marcus whispered in my ear, "This is much more fun than a movie, don't you think?"

I nodded as Nate pulled away from me slightly, kissing

down my neck. I leaned against Marcus's chest, feeling him cover my back with his body while his hands crept up beneath my shirt to hold my breasts, gently playing with my nipples.

Nate's hands moved up from my hips, a featherlight touch dancing along the seam of my shorts before popping off the button. "If you need to stop or slow down at all, you tell us, okay?"

Breathlessly, I gave him a swift nod. "I will. But until then, don't you dare stop. Either of you."

Marcus chuckled in my ear and the sound went straight to my panties. "Yes, ma'am."

With a quick tug, Nate pulled down my shorts, dragging my panties with them. "Oops. Didn't actually mean to get those off you so quickly, but I won't complain." He shrugged before kissing me again, hungrier than before, and stroking his fingers along the wet seam of my pussy. His kisses turned to nibbles, moving across my jaw to my earlobe, and I held on to one of each of their shoulders to steady myself.

As they each kissed a side of my neck, mirroring each other, my brain worked to form the question that had been floating around my mind since they'd sandwiched me between them in Moonlit Magicks. "So, y'know how you said the two of you, um, sleep together sometimes?"

Marcus ground his hips between my ass cheeks, letting me feel the hard length of him against me through his clothes. "Mm, we do. Why do you ask? Have you been picturing us?"

"I think she has, she's soaked down here," Nate murmured against my skin while he started to work his fingers inside me.

"Can... Can I watch you?" My cheeks burned as I got

the words out. I'd always had trouble saying what I wanted from partners, but the two of them made me want to say it.

"Oh, we can definitely arrange that. Tell me, what do you think we were doing while you were busy in that cave yesterday?"

My eyes widened, meeting Nate's intense gray gaze. "Were you...?"

Marcus groaned against my neck, grinding his hips harder. "Seeing you with Erich got me all kinds of frustrated. So our dear Nathaniel offered to help me take the edge off, so to speak."

Nate licked across his lower lip with a wink, brushing his thumb against my clit in time with the strokes of his fingers. Marcus noticed my legs starting to shake and wrapped an arm around my waist, holding me up while his other hand reached around to cup my jaw and tilt my head towards him. His lips met mine in a bruising kiss, muffling my moans as Nate stroked me into a toe-curling climax between them.

As I slowly came down from my high, I rested my head back against Marcus's shoulder. Nate removed his glistening fingers from me, holding them up to his familiar's lips. Marcus grinned wickedly as he licked a long line up Nate's hand, catching my lingering juices on his tongue before sealing his lips over Nate's fingers, licking them clean.

Before I could attempt to form words about how hot that was, Nate leaned forwards slightly, catching me in a kiss that had me gripping his shoulders to steady myself. He pulled away once Marcus released his fingers with a wet 'pop' sound.

Looking down at me, he spoke in a deep voice that had my insides weak in anticipation. "Let's move to the bedroom. I don't like the idea of Bailey and Ellis coming home to see you like this."

Marcus chuckled behind me. "Good call. Why don't you head up to your room, I'll be there in a minute." He gently lowered me back to my feet and gave me a quick smooch on my neck before picking up my discarded clothes and dashing to his own bedroom.

Nate led the way up to his room with me following in only my shirt. My bare butt hung out, just waiting for Bailey or Ellis to come home and see me half-streaking through their house with their roommates. We made it to Nate's room, quickly followed by Marcus, who was carrying a box of condoms and a bottle of lube.

Noticing my glance at that, he winked at me. "Oh, don't worry, Flower Power, that one's not for you. You asked for a show, after all."

An excited grin spread across my face. "What are you planning?"

"Trust us." He cupped my face in his hands and kissed me deeply, instantly making me regret my lack of panties. "Now just entertain yourselves for a few minutes while I get ready."

I turned back to Nate, who had stripped down to his boxers while I was distracted. Running my fingers through his pale blonde hair, I pulled him down for another kiss. I tugged lightly on his hair, making him moan into my mouth. I moved one hand down to the waistband of his boxers, pushing it down and feeling his cock spring free against my belly.

"Lie on the bed, Nate?" I asked between kisses. "I want to take you in my mouth."

"As if I'd say no to that," he murmured against my lips before moving to the bed, kicking his boxers off fully before lying next to where Marcus kneeled near the headboard, naked. "Nearly ready for me?"

Marcus shivered, his eyes unfocused as he slowly moved two lubed fingers in and out of his ass. "Been a little while since I've had you back here, Nate. Give me a few more minutes, would you? Mm, besides I wanna see what our girl can do too."

Taking my cue, I took off my shirt and fluttered my wings a little, letting me hover onto the bed to straddle Nate's legs. I slowly ran my hands up his muscular thighs, leaning down as I moved farther up, until one hand gently held his cock to my mouth. My tongue flicked out over the tip, having a quick taste, before I opened up and sucked the head into my mouth, swirling my tongue around.

Nate's moans echoed around the room, building my confidence to take more of him into my mouth and stroke my hand along where I couldn't reach. I began to bob my head up and down, taking a little more of him each time, until he bumped the back of my throat. Forcing down my gag reflex, I continued to suck, occasionally coming off to give him a long slow lick from base to tip before taking him back in my mouth again. My spare hand cupped his balls as I planted wet kisses up and down his shaft, until an arm wrapped around my waist from behind, pulling me off Nate completely and holding me to a firm chest.

"What the—?"

"Uh-uh. We can't have him finishing in that wicked little mouth of yours." Marcus chuckled, holding my jaw in one hand and running his thumb along my lips. "I still wanna use that dick, if you don't mind."

Nate groaned from the bed, sitting up on his elbows to glare at us. "Marcus, you damn tease!"

"Who, me? I would never!" He batted his eyelashes

innocently, even while holding my naked body to his in a more than compromising position. His long fingers moved down from my waist to tease my opening as he held me close, his own hardness pressing against my ass.

My hips moved against his fingers, seeking more contact, and I groaned as he pulled them away. "You really are a damn tease."

He grinned against my mouth, leaving little kisses along my cheek as he spoke. "I'd only be a tease if I didn't plan on giving you more in just a moment, Flower Power. Now lie back on the bed for me."

Nate moved off the bed to give me room, trailing his fingers down the length of my body as he walked to the end of the bed. He moved behind Marcus, muttering something in his ear I couldn't make out, but it made Marcus bark out a laugh, shaking his head. "Now who's the tease, Nathaniel?"

Using the slick grace of his python, Marcus crawled up the bed, nudging my legs apart and up to my chest until he sat between them. He lifted my hips, stuffing a pillow underneath to angle me up to him, then reached over to the condoms, quickly sheathing himself. Bracing himself on his forearms either side of my head—so as not to crush me or my splayed out wings—he slowly pressed inside of me until our hips were flush against each other.

As I adjusted to the thick sensation of him inside me, he trailed kisses down my neck, nipping his teeth against my skin. One of his hands moved down to circle my clit, making me gasp in a breath and grind my hips. Marcus slowly began to move, working up a rhythm that had my back arching and soft moans leaving my throat.

I felt the moment Nate began to push inside Marcus, his movements stilled inside me for a few moments, then steadily pushed deeper into me from the force of Nate behind him. As Marcus let out a shuddering breath above me, I fisted a hand in his hair while licking along his collarbone to the crook of his neck. I sucked on a spot there, clenching my inner muscles around him a little. I met Nate's half-closed eyes over Marcus's shoulder as I massaged his scalp, loving the soft involuntary noises he made.

Nate grinned down at me, kissing the top of my head over Marcus's shoulder and taking one of my hands in his on the mattress. He gave me a wink before starting up a fierce rhythm into his familiar, who met each of his thrusts and pushed harder into me each time. The noise of slapping skin and heavy breaths filled the room as we each edged closer to our peak.

When Marcus's fingers started massaging my clit again, stars burst from behind my eyes and my toes curled as I moaned my release. My hand squeezed Nate's as my other pulled Marcus's hair in a way I hoped wasn't painful, but I couldn't let go. My walls clenched down on Marcus's cock and he moaned his release in my ear, unable to hold back from the sensations tormenting him from both sides. Nate thrust into him a few more times, but quickly followed us, collapsing to one side of me while Marcus took the other.

We cleaned up quickly, then lay there in relative silence for what felt like forever, curled around each other's sweaty bodies. It felt so right having them on either side of me, though I missed Erich. I wondered if he'd ever be interested in joining in with all of us, but I wouldn't mind keeping him to myself as well. We would see how things go, assuming we still had a home here after tomorrow.

CHAPTER SEVENTEEN

Erich arrived back at the house the next morning with breakfast in one hand and a bag with a change of clothes and toothbrush for me in the other. Apparently, Maeve had dropped the clothes with him on her way out of town for the day with a wink and a crisp high five. I was glad they got along so well, but I was more grateful to have a change of underwear. Two days in the same clothes, even if one of them was spent sleeping, did not smell great.

I was pleasantly surprised to find the hairband Erich had given me was in the bag, washed and dried since our river-swimming adventure in Cupid Falls. Walking downstairs after a shower, in clean clothes and my hair pushed back from my face, I felt ready to take on the world.

The guys were sitting around the breakfast bar, speaking in hushed tones as I approached. I was pretty sure I heard my name mentioned, and I was willing to bet that they knew as much as I did that we needed to take action today. The town couldn't afford to wait any longer.

"Did I miss the meeting?" I asked, only half-joking.

Nate smiled, turning to face me and pulling me between his legs for a chaste kiss. "You haven't missed much. Mostly me trying to work out how to enhance your magic and these two comparing notes."

"Notes?"

Marcus looked up from his whispers with Erich, both of them grinning from ear to ear. "Yeah, notes on what you like. There are three of us, after all, it'd be a waste of an opportunity to not make the most of this."

Coughing to hide my blush and the fact I was desperately resisting the urge to throw off my clothes and run back to bed, I poured myself a mug of coffee, grabbed a bagel from the bag Erich brought, and took a seat next to Nate.

"Were you able to come up with anything? I don't know much about magic boosters, but is there anything at the shop that could help?"

"Oh, Ellis could whip up something like that in a flash, but you'd probably spontaneously combust." Marcus laughed, as though he were reliving a fond memory.

From what I remembered of Ellis and Maeve's chaotic relationship, arson was always a possibility with him.

Nate rolled his eyes. "That was one time, and you know it. Besides, I think I found something safer in one of my great-grandmother's books this morning. It's a way for you to be able to tap into our powers, instead of me just boosting you."

"So I'd be able to hold the connection and end Delwyth's spell?"

"That's the plan. It's totally different from the enhancement I gave you last time. This spell would share all our magic and internal energies between all four of us, so you could harness it, Aggy. You would have all three of us backing you up."

Marcus shook his head, sighing deeply. "Nate, as wonderful as the power of friendship sounds, that just wouldn't work. Those kinds of spells need a foundation to build from, like our familiar bond, or the ties of a witches' coven."

"What about the link of fated mates?" Erich suggested.

Nate grinned. "Exactly. The unique magical bond between the four of us is what makes this possible. We can power you up, Aggy, and help you make things right."

Glancing over to Erich and Marcus, both deep in their own thoughts. I raised an eyebrow. "And you're both okay with this? I mean, neither of you have your own magic to spare."

Marcus sighed, scratching behind his neck in an attempt to look nonchalant. "From what we know, it shouldn't make a difference if we have magic ourselves. This spell is more like a transfer of energy or supernatural abilities, so it should be safe. Like if I were the focus of this spell instead of you, I wouldn't be able to use your magic. Instead, I'd probably just shift into a bigger python or just be a lot stronger or faster. You get the idea. The human would probably end up being some kind of super-soldier."

Erich smiled to himself, imagining the possibilities. "I'd insist on being called Super-Erich and only use my powers for good."

"Whereas I'd go swimming in the loch to piss off that kelpie, then shift into mega-python and finally scare the shit outta him." Marcus cackled at the thought. It had clearly been on his mind for a while.

"I really can't see that working out for you in the long run." I'd met Tase, one of Lex's mates and a bouncer at

Flare, a few times. He was as stubborn as he was creative, and I feared that Marcus would quickly get in over his head if he made the mistake of messing with the kelpie and his territory.

We quickly agreed to head over to the Village Green as soon as we were ready. I hated covering up my wings with Marcus's shirt to walk through town again, but I knew that it wouldn't be for much longer. Guilt ate away at my stomach like a cramp, twisting my insides, knowing what I had to do. But my mother believed I could do this and so did the guys. I wasn't going to let them down.

It was mid-morning by the time we left the house, swiftly moving through the narrow streets towards the Village Green. Even though we avoided the main roads, I'd never seen Moonlit Falls so quiet. It was eerie seeing the streets so empty, but also a relief knowing people were safe from the ward malfunctions.

As we approached my renovation site, I took Erich's hand in mine, smiling as he gave it a reassuring squeeze. Delwyth looked exceptionally large and intimidating in the center of the space. Her thick, twisting branches reached up to a foreboding gray sky. The lush greenery of the leaves seemed dulled by the knowledge of what Delwyth was poisoned by.

Erich pulled me out of my thoughts with another squeeze of my hand. "Hey, it's going to be okay, Aggy. Come on, Nate's already set up."

Burning candles stood spaced out in a small circle on one side of Delwyth, with a small silver bowl in the center next to an ornate blade. It looked like Nate was bringing out the fancy tools for this spell. I had no idea if the prettiness of the equipment affected the quality of spellcasting, but I was willing to try anything at this point.

At Nate's instruction, we each took up a position next to a candle. I took the North spot, representing Earth. Erich took air to the East. Marcus acted as fire to the South, and Nate stood at the West for water.

"I guess it's a good thing I didn't end up with four mates, we'd have run out of room here," I joked awkwardly, trying and immediately failing to lighten the mood. The guys weren't at all amused at the thought of having to deal with another person in the chaos of our newly bonded lives.

"Are you ready?" Nate asked us all.

A thought crossed my mind before I could agree. "This won't turn us all into your harem of familiars, right?"

Nate shook his head. The corner of his mouth curved up in a smirk at that thought. "No, this isn't a bonding like Marcus and I did. That was creating a bond from nothing. This will only tap into an already existing bond, temporarily opening up our magics and energies to each other, to use. You're all safe, except Marcus. He's stuck with me at this point."

Marcus shrugged his shoulders, trying to act aloof, but there was a sparkle of happiness in his amber eyes that showed he liked his life with Nate. Even if they'd had a rocky start at the beginning of their bond, they both belonged together and in our foursome.

"So long as we keep our focus on you, you should be able to draw on our energies the same way Nate can do with me day-to-day. It feels weird, kind of tingly, but it's effective as hell."

"Sounds fun and terrifying all at once. Let's do this." I shrugged out of Marcus's shirt and held out my hand to Nate. His thumb brushed over my palm just like he had on our date, before he swiped the blade across in a quick, thin line. I barely felt the knife kissing my palm before my hand was tilted over the silver bowl, letting the blood drip inside.

I held the bowl up as he worked his way around the circle, letting Erich, Marcus, and then himself bleed into the bowl. We didn't need much blood, and Nate healed each of our cuts with a swift spell. He then plucked one of Delwyth's low hanging leaves and dipped it into the blood.

"Using this should help direct the energy to you, as the Earth element here. Or I may have just pissed off an ancient tree for no reason. Let's find out!"

Using the blood-dipped oak leaf as a brush, Nate dabbed the blood on each of our foreheads, over our third eye, muttering his spells in a low voice. We held hands in the circle as Nate continued his chant, and I could feel the power moving through me. It was wild, like being dragged underwater by a wave and only being able to ride it out until you could gasp for air.

With a final shout, Nate's spell was cast. We each dropped our hands, staggering to stay on our feet. A burst of magic flitted between us, unsure of its true host anymore. It randomly filled me with bursts of energy before dashing to someone else as I struggled to hold on to it.

Nate yelled, "Focus on Agate. The magic will be naturally drawn into her!"

I felt their gazes fixate on me, and the magic followed immediately. My wings flexed and my legs cramped as the magic swirled inside me, refusing to settle. Digging my toes into the soil, I closed my eyes and concentrated on taking slow, deep breaths, giving the magic time to calm down.

The frantic swirling of magic inside me gradually steadied into a pulse that vibrated through me. It was an incredible sensation. Even with my eyes closed, I was aware of everything touching the ground for what felt like miles. I could feel every living thing, down to each individual blade of grass, and even the insects beneath the soil.

Opening my eyes, before I could get overwhelmed by it all, I gave the guys what I hoped was a reassuring smile. "It definitely worked."

Erich paced around in a small circle, his eyes wide with adrenaline. "Yeah, that was a crazy feeling. I'm not ready to be Super-Erich again. How do you feel?"

"Like I'm either going to throw up or fly to Mars with three beats of my wings."

Marcus grinned. "Sounds about right. You've inherited my snake eyes, by the way. They look good on you."

I rolled my new eyes. Of course, Marcus would find his traits attractive on me. Flexing my fingers, ready for what came next, I turned to Nate. "I'm ready."

"That's my Sprite. We'll be right behind you."

With each step I took towards Delwyth, life bloomed beneath my bare feet. The grass around me was suddenly up to my knees, interspersed with wildflowers I'd never planted here myself.

The magic flowing through me was incredibly strong, and it was looking for any way to be used as I moved, so I had to work quickly.

Delwyth's ghostly form appeared as I placed one hand on her bark. I gasped at the sight before me. She looked worse than before, more frail and hunched over in pain, with huge bags under her eyes. The exclusion zone spell was taking every scrap of magic she had, and she clearly didn't have much left.

"It's time, little Sprite. Please help me, before it's too late." Her weak voice croaked out the plea, breaking my heart little by little.

Reluctantly, I nodded and turned away from her spirit

form to grip her bark with both hands. Strangely, I couldn't sense any animals inside the tree. There used to be birds' nests, and even a few squirrels living here not long ago, but they must have already left as Delwyth's internal magic began to perish more rapidly. Animals are always strangely intuitive, and it was a relief to know they were safe.

Digging my feet firmly into the soil, the ground began to shake as I harnessed the swirling magic inside me. Large cracks split the terrain wide open and Delwyth's thick roots began to rise above the ground like snakes reaching up to the sun.

Vines wrapped around my ankles, steadying me from slipping in the moving soil as I pushed my magic harder. As more roots forced their way through crevices to the surface, they slowly started to dissolve into nothingness. I focused the vibrating power out of me, forcing branches to break off and fall from Delwyth's canopy, landing on the ground in crashes, before melting away into the Earth.

Taking a glance back at Delwyth's hovering spirit form, I couldn't help but let my tears flow. This was so wrong. She was smiling, silently cheering me on, even when her form started to fade in and out of sight.

I wanted to save her. I wanted to give her the peaceful life she should have been able to enjoy for the past hundred years.

I didn't want her to go.

With a scream bursting from me, I pushed every scrap of my magic and my intent into Delwyth. Her bark began to break apart beneath my hands, splitting up the center as she fully rose from the ground. Digging my nails into the largest crack, I pulled it apart until a deafening boom erupted out from the tree, ripping my ankles from the vines and sending me flying back into my mates.

Strong arms grabbed me in mid-air, pulling me to safety, and shielding me from the huge wave of magic blasting out into the town and beyond.

I slowly forced my eyes to open as the ringing in my ears slowly subsided. I could just about make out Marcus yelling from above me. "Hey, hey! You okay? Agate!"

Waving my hand, I shooed Marcus away so I could sit up on my elbows. Nate and Erich rushed over. "I'm okay, really. Is Delwyth...?"

My voice trailed off as I looked over the area. Gaping crevices littered the ground and in the center was nothing. Just an empty space where a magnificent oak tree once stood.

"I did it." The words were positive, but the victory was hollow.

Taking Nate's offered hand, I stood up on shaking feet. The magic I'd had moments ago dissipated in my successful uprooting of Delwyth. My eyes roamed over the ruins of my garden as I shuffled forwards slowly. A small noise, like a whimper, caught my attention, and my head spun to one of the cracks.

A pale hand reached out of the crack, and I couldn't hold back the gasp that burst from me when a head appeared above the soil.

"Delwyth?" I croaked out.

My guys clearly had better reactions than I did. They quickly moved to help a very solid, human-looking, and very naked, Delwyth from the crevice. She looked just as she had in her spirit form: old, quite frail, but with a determination in her eyes I hoped I could muster myself.

"Oh, she's nude. She's very nude. Clothes!" Erich babbled in a panic, averting his eyes.

"On it!" Marcus stripped down to his underwear in

record time, passing a shirt and pair of jeans to her, before shifting into his python form smoothly, curling around my ankles.

Delwyth looked at the clothes and rolled her eyes. "Really? I've been naked for centuries! What difference does this form make?"

Erich coughed loudly, his eyes still firmly focused on the sky. "Well, in this one you might get arrested by Officer Stone for public indecency."

She scoffed and reluctantly pulled the shirt over her head and dragged the jeans on, rolling them at the ankle a few times. Nate moved to stand next to me, letting Marcus slither up his body and drape himself over his shoulders. Nate's eyes were wide with shock plastered over his face.

"Aggy, she's... You didn't... How?"

I grinned, the joyful reality of everything finally setting in. "All I know is I wasn't thinking of destroying her. I wanted to protect her. That's all I've ever wanted for her."

"And you've succeeded, little Sprite." Delwyth smiled at us all in turn. "The raw power of a blood witch, the heart of a human, the form-changing abilities of a shifter, the connection of an Earth sprite. The combination is unheard of. I'm very lucky you had access to these magics."

"So instead of the combo-magic destroying you, it gave you a new life as a human?" Erich asked, finally able to look her in the eye now she had clothes on.

"Oh no, child. I feel as though after a long rest, I would be able to return to my previous form at will."

"You're an Oak Tree Shifter?" Nate asked, his eyebrows raised in shock. I'd heard of a few tree shifters before, but they were rare. The most recent sightings were Maple Tree shifters near Silver Springs.

"Yes, that's what my magic tells me. Though I think I'll

use this form for a while. I rather like the idea of exploring the town, maybe even going farther eventually. I doubt I'll ever permanently return to this spot. Life does get rather dull being in one space for centuries on end. I'll need somewhere to stay in the meantime, though. You'll help me, won't you, little Sprite?"

Did a tree just become my new roommate?

CHAPTER EIGHTEEN

As the next few days passed, I fell into a sort of routine with the guys. I was working long hours through the day with Maeve, determined to make the Village Green as beautiful as possible in Delwyth's absence. It had taken a full day to repair all the damage I caused from uprooting her. We were lucky none of the furniture had arrived from my beaver-shifter friend yet.

I still didn't have the heart to fill in the place where she'd once stood so majestically, since she now stood on very human feet in my spare bedroom. So, I'd worked around that spot for now.

The guys had been keeping me busy, too. I was getting to know Nate and Marcus better each day, and felt so at ease around them both. I visited them at Moonlit Magicks for lunch most days, and they were talking about finding a more permanent home in town. They mentioned it to me cautiously, like they were gauging my reaction, and I think they were quietly planning on somewhere for all four of us in the future.

Surprisingly, I was excited by the idea. I didn't know if

I'd want to leave my treehouse with Maeve and our new roommate anytime soon, but I liked the potential.

Now that Erich knew about supernaturals, he was making a huge effort to become part of the magical community. Once he'd downloaded Screech, it was hard to tear him away from his phone. He hadn't realized how many of his friends were hidden supes, and he loved finally understanding why one of his friends never wanted to go out on sunny days. We were all planning on taking him for a night out in Flare soon so he could see the unfiltered wild side of the locals.

"How's this, Aggy?" Erich asked me, holding up one of my favorite succulents by the roots.

Maeve had taken Delwyth out for a tour of the town, now that she felt strong enough to walk around, leaving Erich and I alone in the house. He'd shown some interest in my houseplants and was kind enough to help me while he was off work. Unfortunately, he had no trace of a green thumb whatsoever.

"That's, uh... better, but you need to tease the roots out more. They're still all clumpy, here." I carefully put down the newly potted jade plant I was raising to be given as a gift by one of Jade's mates, and took the succulent from Erich. His eyes followed my movements as I showed him the technique again, gently teasing the roots with my fingers until large lumps of dirt fell on the table between us.

Erich slouched in his seat, defeated. "Easy for you to say. You've got magic for this stuff."

"No magic here, sorry. Just dirty hands." I smirked at him. I'd clearly been spending too much time with Marcus. "I'm actually surprised you're so bad at this. Those fingers usually work wonders with me."

Erich doubled over in a wheezing laugh, like I'd punched him in the gut.

"Anyway, try again with one of the aloe vera. Goddess knows we have enough of it. I should give some away at some point." I pondered the thought as I scanned over the potted chaos of the living room until I realized Erich was speaking to me. "Huh? Sorry, I zoned out."

"No worries. It's cute when you get in the zone like that. But I was asking when you think you'll be finished with the Village Green renovation."

I'd been avoiding this topic for days, but it had only been a matter of time before I was asked outright. "It's, um... it's almost done. I just need to find something to fill in the center space. I hadn't exactly planned on uprooting the main attraction and letting her move in with me when I started."

Erich took my hand in his, entwining our dirt-encrusted fingers. "Oh, you'll think of something. The Village Green will be back open before you know it, better than ever."

"I know, you're right. But at this point I'll settle for throwing a nice-looking boulder into the space and calling it a day." I forced a laugh, only half-joking. I really was clueless what to do with the space Delwyth's tree form had stood. I'd considered different trees, statues, topiaries, even a small pond, but nothing felt quite right to me.

A knock at the front door pulled me out of my thoughts. I shooed Erich back into his seat as he started getting up to answer. "I got it, don't worry. You just stay here and practice not maiming my poor plants."

"Hey, I'm doing my best!" he whined.

Danburite's smiling face greeted me as I opened the door. Her blonde hair fell in soft curls past her shoulders as she waved, leaves and little black scales falling to the ground with her movement. "Hello, Aggy! Do you have a few minutes?"

"Yeah, of course. I haven't seen you in forever." I stepped aside to let her in but she shook her head, motioning for me to join her outside.

"I actually need to show you something, over here." She led me outside, grinning to herself. "Do you remember those acorns you helped me pick last fall?"

I remembered. Dani hadn't explained why at the time, but she'd been looking into the lifespan of oak trees. We agreed that Delwyth should be left alone, but we would try growing fresh from her acorns. Unfortunately, we never had any success. Despite our best efforts, most of them withered, and we never figured out what caused it. Dani moved on to try other things, and I didn't give it much thought afterwards.

"The ones we couldn't get to grow?"

"That is the thing, one of them never died. I do not know why, maybe we did something to it last year, but it has never grown, or withered, or done anything, until the other day. Look!"

My jaw dropped. Next to my mailbox was a large plant pot with a lush, green sapling poking out from the soil. "Is that..."

"I have had to change the pot twice already. The growth is crazy for only a few days!" Dani squealed.

"Dani, this is incredible!" I kneeled next to the pot and gently brushed a small leaf with the back of one of my fingers. A familiar, calming energy washed over me, and I could have cried from the sheer joy bursting out of my heart.

The energy of the plant matched Delwyth's.

"The magic shop owners told me what happened to the

tree we picked the acorns from. Delwyth, right?" Dani kneeled beside me, admiring the sapling. "I think it would be good to plant this little one in her place."

As much as I wanted to cry and hug her, I had to stop myself. "But you needed this, didn't you?"

Dani shrugged. "I think you need it more than I do. I will figure something out. You need not worry!"

I couldn't hold back anymore. Squeezing Dani tightly, I cried out all the joy in my body. Dani held me a bit awkwardly. We were friends, sure, but this was probably a bit much for her. I couldn't help it, though. Even though Delwyth herself was alive and well, seeing her missing from the Village Green had felt so wrong to me. This little sapling held so much potential for what the garden would be once again.

"Okay, you are okay." She patted me awkwardly on the back until I started to calm down to a light sniffle. "Feel better?"

"So much better." I stood up, dusting the dirt off my knees. "Come on, we should get her planted back in the Village Green as soon as we can."

Dani looked at me, her head tilted in confusion. "Sure, but do you really need me there?"

Wiping my eyes with the heel of my hand, I smiled brightly. "I want you there. You're the whole reason this sapling exists! I'll call the guys too. I wanna get this little bud checked over before she goes in the ground."

I couldn't risk any remnant of the exclusion spell being on the sapling. The council might be able to apply a new one in a more stable manner, but I didn't want any trace of the original spell near her.

While Dani waited with the plant pot, I rushed inside and grabbed Erich. I gave him a brief explanation of what had happened, then texted Nate, Marcus, and Maeve to come meet us. We moved quickly, taking it in turns to carry the oversized plant pot into town. I was impressed that Dani had managed to carry it to my house by herself. It was huge for a sapling. Nate and Marcus were already waiting for us by the time we made it to the Village Green, and had also dragged Bailey and Ellis along for the ride.

Maeve arrived not long after us with Delwyth. I still had to do a double-take every time I saw her in her human form. Like me, she liked to walk around barefoot, and had a fondness for loose clothing. Well, that was when she wore clothing at all. She had refused to wear anything for the first couple of days living with us, saying that clothes were "unnatural" and she'd been naked her whole life. She had a point, but there were only a few naked bodies I could stand to look at before my morning coffee.

"Good, the gang's all here." I grinned, my heart pounding from the mix of excitement and heavy lifting. "I need everyone with magic to check for any lingering enchantments or spells anchored to this plant. There's probably going to be a few growth charms, but those are harmless. I can regulate the growth once it's in the ground."

"I'll just stand here and look pretty with the human, shall I?" Marcus asked with a wink.

"You do make a wonderful sight together, but feel free to shout some words of encouragement."

"Woo. Go team."

"I'll take it."

Nate grinned at me, and I could tell that he was pleased to see me in my element. He poked his thumb with the needle-blade on his keys and rubbed the droplet of blood into one of the leaves. Maeve and Dani took up a position either side of him and each placed a hand on the stem of the plant, eyes closed in concentration. Ellis pinched some of the dirt between his fingers and dropped it into a vial he pulled out of a pocket. As he added a liquid from a second vial, Bailey waved a hand over the plant in a pattern I didn't recognize.

Delwyth stood next to me as we watched them. It was incredible to see so many different kinds of magic coming together to try and protect this small life, and I could tell she was happy to see one of her children had managed to gain life.

Maeve was the first to step back, so I took her place beside Nate and dug my fingers deep into the soil. My wings twitched as I spread my magic over the plant, searching for everything I could possibly find.

As predicted, there were the growth spells Dani and I had placed on the acorns last year. They felt safe, so I moved on. I found a new protection spell that felt like it had been placed by Dani once it had started to sprout, but then there was nothing. As hard as I searched, I couldn't find any trace of the exclusion-zone spell that had been on Delwyth.

Nate spoke next to me. "I think it's safe, Aggy. The spell didn't transfer to her seeds."

Erich sighed in relief. "That's good to hear. Otherwise we'd have had exclusion zones everywhere if they'd been planted."

Delwyth nodded, a serious look furrowing her brow. "You're correct. I was very careful, even with that wretched spell attached to me."

She was right. "Most trees want to spread out and let their children grow. Delwyth wasn't like that, even in her tree form. My best guess is that now she's not holding in all her magic, it was free to move to her seedlings and this was the only one left. This is her only child, just waiting to awaken in the ground."

I felt a hand at my back, stroking gently between my wings. Marcus kissed the top of my head and spoke softly. "Then let's not keep it waiting. I want it to start talking to you so I can name it Leafer Sutherland."

"What about Aracorn?" Erich asked.

"Don't be silly, just look at it. It's clearly Adam Treevine." Nate grinned while Ellis clapped him on the back.

"No, it needs a name to grow into. Chuck Forest."

"It looks more like a Leaves Buscemi to me," Bailey commented, not even trying to hold back the smirk that told me he knew exactly how much this irritated me.

Maeve rolled her eyes. "You boys really need to branch out with these puns."

"Oh my Goddess, seriously? You're all children, and since I'm only obligated to put up with three of you idiots, the rest of you better hush right up!" I yelled as loudly as I could, satisfied when they each awkwardly shuffled away apologetically.

Delwyth gave me a proud smile, clearly glad I'd stood up for her sapling.

As I pulled Maeve and Dani over to help me plant the sapling, I couldn't hold back the thought that popped into my head. Pushing down the guilt, I whispered in Maeve's ear, "Morgan Treeman."

EPILOGUE

The re-opening of the Village Green was everything I'd hoped for, and more. Little Morgan the sapling was growing quickly, already taller than Marcus, though still on the skinny side. It would be a few years before she grew to the size Delwyth had been, even with the spells helping things along.

I'd told everyone that the name Morgan was a fairly common name for girls back home, which was true, and kept the origin of her name a secret. Only Maeve knew the truth, and I'd sworn her to secrecy.

Delwyth and I regularly took walks into town to check in with Morgan and see how she was getting on. It was cute seeing Delwyth as a mother to the new oak tree. Morgan was easily one of the most talkative trees I've met. She was so curious about the town and its residents. Part of me wondered if I could turn her into an oak shifter like her mother, but I kept that thought to myself. The magic required was too powerful and uncontrollable. I wasn't sure I could do it again. Besides, Morgan seemed content so far, like most trees.

Nate finally got an appointment to speak to the Paranormal Council about the ward exclusion spell, and they were unsurprisingly oblivious to the whole thing. He did manage to get them to agree to only use temporary exclusion spells in the coming years, to prevent it happening again. So it was a win overall. Officer Stone was especially happy about the ruling, after he'd spent almost a week doing overtime helping to hide the effects of magic from humans. Poor guy really needed a break.

Plans were already being prepared for the next Halloween ball, and I was determined to go with my mates this year. The rumor going around town was that it would be an outdoor event to celebrate the Village Green, and I hoped it was true. I was practically soaring with excitement to cover the garden with jack-o'-lanterns and set up some games for the locals.

Speaking of locals, the renovation was a huge hit. From my spot next to Morgan, I could see Lex had brought Newt over for the opening, and Tase looked like he was trying to use the kid as an accomplice for a prank opportunity against the selkies. I made a mental note to warn him off ruining my work, but it looked like Colbie had that covered for me. She scolded Tase like she was his mother. I almost felt bad for him.

I spotted Laz having a full conversation with some squirrels in a tree next to the gazebo, while her ferret shifter mate scurried around her legs in his animal form. It looked like the ferret had attracted the curiosity of Dee, a tree nymph I hadn't spoken to for a while, but her friend Vivianite was pulling her away gently by the arm to grab some drinks.

Jasper had brought the local summer camp kids over for

the opening, and they were loving the space. While some of them attended a Spanish lesson from Rob—though it could have been a pirate lesson, for all I knew—the rest completely took over the swings and climbing frames. They were now free to use their powers with humans completely oblivious to their actions.

"Did you see that kid just turn into a skunk?!"

Well, most of them. My favorite human was now a permanent addition to the supe-community in his own way. Erich looked especially good today. He'd traded his regular delivery driver uniform for a Screech delivery driver uniform. Working for the supernatural app really made him feel like he was supporting our community in town. He'd only had the job a few days, but he said it was far more fun than the human-run service.

Marcus sighed, massaging his temple with one hand. "You've seen my python form how many times now? And you're still amazed by a damn *skunk*?"

Wrapping my arms around his waist, I pulled my shifter into a *cwtch*. "Oh, don't pout. The novelty will wear off soon... probably."

Slinging an arm around my shoulders, Marcus herded Erich and I towards the picnic tables where Nate waited with our group. Ellis and Bailey's other roommates had finally returned to town from visiting their families, which meant Nate and Marcus had been relocated to the apartment above Moonlit Magicks for the time being.

Alaric was a muse working as an art teacher in the local high school, and Drew was a shifter working as a history teacher. I hadn't figured out his animal yet, and apparently he didn't like to tell people about it. The guys all kept quiet about it, so I didn't push, but I was really curious. Even

Maeve didn't know, and she'd dated his best friend for months until last year.

We sat around the picnic area, with drinks provided by Nessie's Pub and ice cream from Bee's, until the sun went down and those with kids headed home. The rest of us waited for the Nightly Vamps show to start up from the gazebo. Their music reminded me of my first date with Nate. Most romances have a song, but we had a whole band.

The lanterns I'd set up around the gazebo looked magical at this time of night, and I couldn't help being proud of myself. Everything here looked perfect. The hedges neatly framed the space, with stone pathways lined with daffodils winding around. The fruit trees were in bloom a little early, thanks to my magic, and the whole space was covered in lush color.

As I sat between my three mates, unexpected as they were, I wondered about my next big project. Maeve warned me to take a break for a while and stick to general maintenance, but word spread quickly in Moonlit Falls. I'd already had a few new job offers around town to consider.

But maybe a vacation was needed? *Mam* had asked me to visit home, and I was pretty sure she knew about my mates, even if she was unaware of the details. She wasn't subtle about asking after them on the phone call we'd had earlier. I needed to make the trip home before she got any ideas about coming here. I wasn't sure I was ready for the embarrassment.

Pretty soon, the band was in full swing and groups of people were dancing without a care in the world. The owner of Betta Fishin' was getting pretty close to Maeve, but I'd heard that Beau would flirt with just about anyone single. Maeve wasn't the girl to calm that guy down, but someone needed to.

Citrine was showing off her dance moves with vigor, until Mikey accidentally spilled his drink down her back, making her sprout hair all over her body in shock. But just one apologetic smooch later, the dance moves were back, fluffy hair and all. It was cute seeing her so happy.

Reaching up to shout over the band in Nate's ear, I decided to ask, "Do you think we could slip away soon?"

He looked down at me with a raised eyebrow, confused as to why I'd want to go, but quickly took the hint when I kissed that spot just below his ear that he loved. I'd been slowly building a mental list of all the guys' weak spots—besides the obvious—that I could use when I wanted something. Not often enough that they knew I was doing it on purpose, but enough that I knew it would be effective.

Nate quickly grabbed Marcus and Erich by their collars, dragging them from the dance floor with the frantic haste of a man who knew he was about to get lucky.

We were back at the apartment above Moonlit Magicks within minutes, after Nate fumbled with the keys for too long and gave up, using a quick spell to open the door and get us inside in record time.

"Aww, is the blood witch distracted by the blood going south? The irony is beautiful," Marcus teased as he followed us upstairs.

"You'd be distracted too if you had her doing that ear-kiss thing she does to me!" Nate motioned to me, laughing.

"And here I thought I was being subtle back there." I chuckled awkwardly as Erich's arms wrapped around me from behind, pulling me back into a hug.

"Nope. We're on to your games. We just decided not to tell you because we like it when you show us what you want." Erich kissed my cheek, his hands teasing along the neckline of my dress.

I turned in his arms, grinning up at him. "Does this mean you're joining us for some group fun?"

He nodded, holding me close and capturing my lips in a soft kiss that made my knees weak. Erich always had this way of being so gentle with me, but still had the same passion that Nate and Marcus had when they were a little rougher.

"Yeah, let's see what I've been missing out on. But I don't think I'm up for any sword crossing just yet. No offense, guys. There's plenty of time for that later if I feel like it."

Nate smiled. "None taken."

Marcus paused in his undressing to fold his arms in a pretend-sulk. "Some taken. I've heard from Flower Power what you can do and I'm curious."

Erich opened his mouth for a comeback, but I quickly covered his mouth with my own to get us back on track. I had plans for tonight. We'd celebrated success in town; now it was time for something more private. And there was nobody else I would rather celebrate with than my kind, hot, and beautifully naked mates.

Thank you for reading MOONLIT AGATE! We hope you loved Aggy and her mates. The story continues in MAGICAL REED

Want to know how Marcus and Nate became bonded? Look out for TWISTED FATE: A Moonlit Agate prequel!

Sign up for Katherine's newsletter to find out about new books!

Turn the page to find out more about Moonlit Falls...

UP NEXT...
A SPELLED LATTE HELPS TWELVE OTHER
WOMEN IN MOONLIT FALLS FIND THEIR
OWN FATED MATES!

MOONLIT DANBURITE

CURSES! Why does it always have to be curses? I can't afford a distraction right now, but when my pet Arach, a sexy Jinn, and a clumsy druid end up my mates, I might be willing to make an exception. But if we can't reverse this curse, we'll never get to do the dirty ever again...

MOONLIT DIAMOND

It's opening day for my candle shop and a Cop, a bookaholic, and a sweet-talking fisherman are all up in my business. A copy-cat is pilfering goods and my spider is keeping secrets. What's a pink-haired ex-thief to do?

MOONLIT VIVIANITE

I never know what I'll get with emergency plumbing calls, but I didn't expect three men claiming to be my mates and asking me to help exorcise a ghost. I could really use a bubble bath about now, but between the poltergeist and the merman all the tubs are taken.

MOONLIT SPINEL

What's a Unicorn got to do around here besides watch your ex trip off a stage in a nightclub? I definitely couldn't tell you. But Fate stepped in as it tends to do. Instead of lions and tigers and bears, I've got mystery men, an ex-girlfriend, and a flooding fountain... Oh my!

MOONLIT SODALITE

When a hunt goes sideways I end up with a vampire whose stake my kitsune would love to examine. Will my crazy libido get in the way when not one, but three men claim to be my mates? My name is Sodalite and shit is about to get real.

MOONLIT NEPHRITE

My ex said I was a failure. I proved him wrong by opening a magical cafe. When it might get shut down, can my four fated mates help save it? Click here to read Moonlit Nephrite now.

MOONLIT ALEXANDRITE

A kelpie, a fire salamander, and a satyr watch me walk into a bar. My succubus wants to keep them, but can I do that and open my craft shop? Someone out there says no.

UP NEXT...

MOONLIT GARNET

I moved to Moonlit Falls to escape my past and reconnect with my family. When the past comes knocking, can my mates help keep me safe? I'm Garnet and we're about to get sucked into a wild adventure that we didn't see coming!

MOONLIT JADE

I've never had a serious relationship ... Like ever. Suddenly three hunky men claim to be my mates. My lucky day, right? It would be if they knew about each other.

MOONLIT CITRINE

Bigfoot walks into a coffee shop and picks up four mates. One wants me, one can't decide, one friend zoned me, and one disappeared. I just want a family dang it. But with the way things are going, it may just be me and my nuggets

MOONLIT JASPER

I'm a rejected mate. That's it. Love life over. So why can't I get these three guys out of my head? Is it possible to have a second chance? With an overprotective dragon on one shoulder, and the Goddess of Chaos on the other, I really hope I can find out.

MOONLIT LAZULITE

My pet grooming salon is getting an update, but the men I hired are flirting with me and my dogs started talking. My name is Lazulite and life just got all kinds of hairy.

UP NEXT...

WE RECOMMEND READING MOONLIT FALLS IN ORDER.

Up next is... Moonlit Danburite Curious about Agate's friend who helped cast the growth spell? Then you'll love her book. One-click MOONLIT DANBURITE now.

WANT TO BE A VIP?

Moonlit Falls is a sister town to the paranormal reverse harem small town of Silver Springs.

Subscribe to the Moonlit Falls newsletter for new release announcements, bonus content, and freebies.

Join our Silver Springs & Moonlit Falls VIP community to stay up to date with new releases and access exclusive stories, bonus scenes, giveaways, and more.

Join the Moon Dust Library Facebook Group for exclusive giveaways and sneak peeks of future books.

You can also join the Silver Springs Library Facebook group to hang out with more quirky, hilarious reverse harem authors and readers.

ALSO BY KATHERINE ISAAC

Moon Dust Library

Twisted Fate - Moonlit Agate MM prequel

(Available 11 November 2021)

Magical Reed (Coming 2022)

Other Titles

Fearless (Charity anthology available 8 September 2021)

Magic and Mayhem Anthology (Coming 2022)

ABOUT THE AUTHOR

Katherine Isaac lives and works in Wales with her beloved cat-son. Growing up surrounded by mythology and history has fueled her love for epic stories of magic, mystery, and romance.

She is happiest with her nose in a book, pinned down by a cat, or surrounded by nature; whether that's lying on the grass or diving in the ocean.

Katherine describes herself as an eternally sleep-deprived pixie, with the mouth of a sailor and too many characters living in her brain.

ACKNOWLEDGMENTS

I can't believe I wrote a book! WOW! Thank you all for reading my very first book baby, Moonlit Agate! It's been a crazy ride getting to this point and I'm so grateful to you all for taking a chance on Agate and her guys. I hope you stick around for more adventures of the people who live in my head!

A huge thanks to all the authors and organizers of Moon Dust Library. You've been a wonderful source of chaos, inspiration, and support throughout the writing process and I couldn't have done this without you all.

To my editor, Emma, and proofreader, Katie, thank you for helping me embrace commas and making my characters shine. Also, thank you to Josie for the stunning cover! You all made this book the best it could be.

Thank you to my lovely Alpha and Beta readers for all your feedback and comments that kept me going.

A special thanks to Susan for outright telling me when I was being a boob and things didn't make sense. I love you and your brain. Our hours of supportive rants and tree-puns have created something pretty neat, if I do say so myself.

Lastly, to anyone who actually reads the acknowledgements: thank you. You're the real heroes.

Printed in Great Britain
by Amazon